ATLANTA
EXTREME

D0556927

ATLANTA EXTREME

RANDY WAYNE WHITE

WRITING AS CARL RAMM

OPEN ROAD

INTEGRATED MEDIA

NEW YORK

Cover design by Andy Ross

ISBN: 978-1-5040-3522-4

This edition published in 2016 by Open Road Integrated Media, Inc.
180 Maiden Lane
New York, NY 10038
www.openroadmedia.com

ATLANTA EXTREME

ONE

The woman who met him at the Fort George Hotel in Belize City, Belize, Central America, told him that she was a whore. She said it with a toss of her head, a quick, penetrating glare of contempt, an expression of aloof indifference that effectively communicated that she didn't give a good goddamn what James Hawker thought of her, anyway, so why try to hide anything?

Hawker sat at the bar and studied the label on the bottle of beer he was drinking. Belikin Beer, Belize Brewing Company, Ltd. Nice drawing of a Mayan ruin on the label. Hawker had studied many labels of many varied beers in the last year. He had been traveling almost continually. When a man is being hunted by the United States Central Intelligence Agency, travel becomes a way of life.

For the last two months he had been living in a seaside estate in Puerto Cabello, not far from Caracas, Venezuela. In South and Central America, Hawker had discovered, a man is asked only one question of importance: Can you pay? If that question is answered satisfactorily, there are no more questions. On the strength of his portfolio at the Swiss bank of Grand Cayman Island, Hawker had always answered satisfactorily.

So lately he had been living the fast, elaborate life of the wealthy American expatriate. Rented villas overlooking the sea. Maids and man-servants. Invitations to strange, formal dinner parties peopled with swarthy men in white tuxedos and beautiful, dangerous-looking women. It was the kind of life that international spies lived. And escaped Nazis. And international drug runners. And businessmen from places like Toledo or Dubuque who embezzle the cream off the second set of books, abandon the wife and kids, and run off with the gum-chewing secretary.

But it was not James Hawker's kind of life. He had had enough of isolation. He had had enough of cryptic conversations with people he did not trust and did not like. He had ridden with too many lunatic women in fast sports cars and bedded enough Latin beauties to last a lifetime.

Hawker had had enough of running and enough of living the soft life. That's why now, now for the first time in months, he was happy. He was happy because he had another mission.

Hawker put the bottle of beer on the counter and considered the woman who sat next to him. She was of the long, lithe, tropical variety: finely grained mahogany skin; pale brown eyes; a touch of Mayan ancestry in the high cheekbones; a blend of slave ancestry in the ripe hips and jutting breasts; a solid dash of Spanish-European in the delicate nose, mouth, and the dark spill of black hair that framed the beautiful duskiness of her face. Her speech was articulate, accented with Spanish, but touched with the cool English of British boarding schools, not the inarticulate street slur of Belize. And the white blouse, tropical-print skirt, and gold jewelry she wore all had the crisp aura of money. If she was a whore, Hawker decided, she was a damn expensive whore.

Hawker said, "I came to Belize because it was my understanding that Colonel Wellington Curtis of Atlanta, Georgia, was going to meet me here. At the bar of the Fort George Hotel. At eight P.M. on this particular Tuesday in June. It is now eight twenty-three P.M., and I really don't care if you are a whore or a secretary or a prima ballerina. All I am asking is: Why did Colonel Curtis send a messenger instead of meeting me as had been arranged? Why did he send you?"

Again the woman's dark eyes flashed at him. "You are disappointed, Mr. Hawker? Perhaps the colonel was thinking of your comfort. You have had a long journey from Venezuela. For reasons with which I am unfamiliar, it was inappropriate for you to fly by commercial airline or, for that matter, to travel under your real name. So you have spent the last two days in small bush planes—I know how cramped and hot they are—and cheap hotels. The colonel told me that his inquiries about you indicate that you are a man who, when he relaxes, prefers to relax with women." Her lips formed a condescending smile. "Perhaps the colonel wishes you to relax before your meeting with him. Perhaps that is why he sent his whore as messenger."

Hawker nodded and took a sip of his beer. "If that's the

reason you're here, then the colonel has wasted your time and mine. I have been sufficiently . . . relaxed during my months in South America. I need no more relaxation. I need only to see the colonel."

"You do not find me attractive?" Without taking her eyes from Hawker the woman opened an ornate gold case and put a cigarette between her lips. When Hawker made no move to light the cigarette for her, she fumbled for a small lighter and added, "Or perhaps the inquiries the colonel made about you were misleading. Perhaps you do not like women."

Hawker noted that her hands shook slightly as she lit the cigarette. He also noticed that she snapped the lighter closed too firmly, as if to compensate for her momentary lack of control. Hawker replied calmly, "You do not understand, Laurene—that is your name, isn't it? Laurene Catocamez? I'm here on business. Whether I find you attractive or not is immaterial. What's important is what I have to say to Colonel Curtis. And what I have to say can't wait for a recreational roll in the hay with you, which, frankly, I wouldn't accept even if there was time."

The woman blew a funnel of smoke and tapped the cigarette on an ashtray, her eyes narrowing slightly. "I see," she said. "You seem to be a man who appreciates frankness, Mr. Hawker, so I hope you do not mind if I am now frank with you. I have not been sent to Belize just to entertain you. I have been sent to interview you before your meeting with Colonel Curtis. The colonel, though he has never met you, knows of your reputation. He has told me about you, for as well as being his whore, I am also his confidante. Colonel Curtis admires your work as an American vigilante. He has heard good things about your wars on the criminals of Los Angeles and Detroit and Washington. As you no doubt know, Colonel Curtis is, in his way, also a vigilante. Though he is an American, he has helped finance, arm, and lead the great rebel cause in my country. He and his mercenaries have fought side by side with my people in a revolution that will not end until the communist regime now in control is destroyed."

"I know," put in Hawker. "In that regard I am in support of the colonel and his work."

"As you should be. Colonel Curtis is a great man. He admires you and your work, too, Mr. Hawker. Even so, he does not know why you want this meeting with him. It is his sincere hope that you have come to offer your considerable abilities to our cause. But Colonel Curtis also knows that his work in Central America has many powerful enemies back in the United States. One of those enemies is Senator Thy Estes, who, according to our sources, is also your lover. The colonel knows that his enemies have been inventing terrible lies about how he gets money to fund this revolution. They have accused him of torture and extortion and God knows what else. Frankly Colonel Curtis wonders if you have come to Central America to assassinate him." Laurene Catocamez gave him a sharp look of appraisal as she inhaled on her cigarette. "Is that why you are here, Mr. Hawker? Have you come to murder Wellington Curtis?"

Hawker couldn't help but smile. He hadn't realized that Curtis, who had been described to him as a Southern aristocrat and military hobbyist, was capable of setting up an intelligence network sophisticated enough to collect such accurate data. Who in the hell besides a few close friends and a couple of airplane pilots knew that he and Thy Estes, the buxom red-headed senator, were lovers? And how many people knew that he was a vigilante? It was an impressive demonstration of Curtis's organization, and Hawker took it for what it was: a warning; a warning that Curtis was more than just a military adventurer.

"You are right, Laurene," Hawker said easily, "I am a man who appreciates frankness. Even so, if I were here to kill Colonel Curtis, you really don't think that I would admit it, do you?"

"Your eyes would tell me what your tongue might not."

"Is that right? You are a mind reader? And what do my eyes tell you now, Laurene?"

The woman studied him carefully, and as she did, Hawker felt, to his surprise, a strong surge of physical desire for her. Perhaps it was the disdain in her manner or the petulant way in which her lips pursed as she stared at him, but the wanting was there: a strong abdominal surge, like pain.

"What do my eyes tell you?" Hawker repeated.

The woman looked deeply into his eyes, and then, after long seconds, seemed to shake herself from a light trance and turned away. "Very little," she said quickly. "Almost nothing."

"Oh? Why is it that I think you're lying?"

The woman pressed her cigarette into an ashtray. "Lying? How absurd. It's really just a trick of mine, you know," she said, smiling for the first time. "I pretend I can read things in people. People love to think someone else knows about them. *Really* knows about them. I guess it gives them a little break in their loneliness. My grandmother was a gypsy. When I tell people this, they immediately believe that I can see into their eyes. They are anxious to accept anything I say about their past or future as true." She laughed. "Of course, I always tell them what they want to hear. It is a trick. My grandmother could do it, though. She really could see into the past. And the future."

"But you can't? You don't have the gift?"

The woman looked at Hawker. "Sometimes," she said slowly. "Sometimes I can see things. Sometimes I have the gift."

"Yet you saw nothing in my eyes."

The woman stood abruptly. "What I saw or did not see does not matter. The future is not ours to control, is it? But I am convinced you have not come to assassinate Colonel Curtis. I do not know why you are here, but I don't think you have come to kill him. That is all that matters. Tomorrow I will take you to him. It is a long journey. You should get some sleep."

"Colonel Curtis isn't here? He's not in Belize?"

"No, he is in Guatemala, in the jungle, near the border of El Salvador and Masagua, where our rebel army trains. He wishes you to see the operation before you pass judgment on him."

"And you are convinced that I haven't already passed judgment?"

"I am satisfied with our interview. It is enough. We will leave at first light."

Without looking at him Laurene Catocamez turned and

walked from the bar. Her hips swung beneath her jet-black hair, and her breasts vibrated tautly, braless, beneath the white blouse as she pushed through the double doors and disappeared.

It was a moment before Hawker realized that before leaving, she had taken the key to his room . . .

TWO

Hawker gave it five minutes, finished his beer, paid the bill. The bartender was a solicitous little man with an earring and a gold tooth. He felt called upon to offer something in return for Hawker's Belizean-dollar tip.

"Your lady very boss, mon. Very boss. She get mad at you, sir? She walk out?"

"She's not my lady—man."

"Not nosy, sir, not nosy. Just trying to help. You need the womans, sir, I be the one to see. I get you fine, clean womans, sir. Very young, very cheap. What you say, sir?"

"I say, why is it that people are trying to supply me with women lately? Do I look that hard-up?"

"Don't understand, sir. Talk plain to old Sam. I get you fine, clean young womans if you want, sir."

Hawker patted the counter. "Not right now, thanks, Sam. Maybe another time."

On the bar's big-screen television Flipper was squeaking and splashing, trying to tell Chip to follow. The satellite dish

11

reception was bad, and it appeared to be snowing on the dolphin, which, in TV land, was king of the sea. No one in the bar was watching, anyway. At a table across the room three Englishmen sat over gin and tonics, discussing their respective banana crops. In the corner, sitting alone, was a huge, bearish black man with a thick black beard and mustache. He was reading a magazine. Near a window that overlooked the fluorescent green of the Caribbean sea, a group of Americans talked of the dangers and demands of their scuba-diving holiday on Ambergris Cay. They talked loudly so that everyone in the bar could hear.

"That damn barracuda was six feet long, no shit, a fucking six-footer, and he came right up to us. Frankie started to panic, but I grabbed his arm and settled him down. Gave him the take-it-easy signal. 'Cudas won't bother you unless you're wearing something shiny, but Frankie really lost his cool when he saw it. Of course, the only place where he's logged any real diving time is Lake Erie. I try to make it down to Florida at least a couple of times a year, so I know how 'cudas act. You have to respect them, but hell, there's no real reason to be afraid of them. A fucking six-footer, no shit . . ."

There were three women at the table and five men. The women, Hawker noted, seemed to be bored by the ongoing macho routine of the men. One of the women was rather pretty in a stocky, blue-eyed Midwestern way, and she smiled at Hawker. Hawker smiled in return and hurried out.

It was a strange mixture of people in a strange country. Belize had the feel of a mud-lot carnival: cheap, gaudy, raw. The country used to be known as British Honduras, a colony of the crown for nearly one hundred and twenty years. But then, in 1981, the United Kingdom granted the country its independence. The local government changed the country's name to Belize while, at the same time, begging the British not to withdraw their troops. The people of Belize knew—as did everyone else—that the Guatemalan army would march in the day after Her Majesty's forces sailed out. The British agreed to stay. As James Hawker trotted down the steps, through the lobby of the hotel and outside, he wondered why the British cared. From what he had seen the people of Belize were lazy, dirty, and undependable. Belize City itself was nothing more than a massive slum built around four or five international banks. In the open markets of the city flies swarmed around squawling black babies while their parents, apparently unconcerned, laughed and danced to American hits on their ghetto blasters. On almost every corner of every block, Rastafarians, in their greasy dreadlocks, hustled drugs: "You want buy good ganjah, mon? Five ounces or five tons, mon, whatever you want. You do the white train, mon? I got good snort; good cocaine. Set you down right nice and easy . . ." The most memorable thing about Belize City was its smell. The city smelled of rotting fruit, bad fish, and the raw sewage that flowed out Haulover Creek, the river that ran past the crowded stilt shacks in the center of town.

Most people came to Belize for the scuba diving off Ambergris Cay or the fishing off the Turneffe Islands. Hawker had come because Colonel Wellington Curtis considered it a country neutral to his cause. His cause was to help the rebels overthrow the government of Masagua, a tiny banana republic wedged in between the troubled nations of Guatemala and El Salvador. Hawker's friend and aide, Jacob Montgomery Hayes, had arranged the meeting after first listing the reasons why Curtis's operation needed to be stopped. Thy Estes had accompanied Hayes, visiting Hawker at his seaside retreat in Venezuela. It was a pleasant reunion for all of them. Hawker hadn't seen Hayes since he had gone renegade (in the opinion of the CIA) and escaped to Ireland. He hadn't seen Thy Estes since he enlisted her aid to help him escape from Belfast, two CIA agents hot on his tail. So at first their meeting had a party atmosphere. Champagne for the senator, American beer for Hawker, and freshly pressed mango juice for Hayes the vegetarian.

But it wasn't long before Hayes got down to business. Hayes was stocky, aesthetic, early sixties, balding; a pipe smoker who was part business tycoon, part Zen Buddhist, part field biologist, part philosopher; an exacting, quiet man whom Hawker admired very much. It seemed like a long, long time ago that Hayes, a billionaire, had offered to finance Hawker on his vigilante operations. Since those days the two men had grown to be much more than just financier and employee. They had become close friends. So Hawker listened quietly as Hayes described Curtis, his operation, and why the operation had to be destroyed.

Hayes began, saying, "Colonel Wellington Curtis—he's an honorary colonel in the Georgia militia, by the way, not a real colonel—is a true Southern aristocrat. His family landed at Jamestown before the Pilgrims. They spread through Virginia and into Georgia. They were plantation owners, slave own-

14

ers; moneyed people who controlled the counties in which they lived and sometimes even the states in which they lived. They fought with distinction in the Civil War and afterward helped rebuild the South through their support of the Democratic Party. The fortune of the Curtis family has dwindled since those times, but even so, Wellington Curtis is a very wealthy man. Most of his wealth was inherited, but he is still an impressive individual, a brilliant historian who has written two classic books on military history: *War Craft*, which is about naval warfare, and *The Killing Tree*, which concerns the Civil War." From a leather briefcase Hayes took two thick volumes and put them on the table. "You may want to read them, James."

Hawker nodded but did not pick up the books. Hayes continued. "About ten years ago Curtis became interested in the conflicts of Central America. It is my understanding that he became interested while doing research for a book he was writing on revolutions. The conflicts of Central America became an absolute passion with him, and before long, he began donating money to the rebel cause in Masagua, a tiny country, which, like Nicaragua, has fallen under Soviet control. Curtis hates communism, just as you and I do. He wrote a brilliant treatise entitled "Lies of the Workers," which every major New York magazine refused to publish. Curtis finally published it and circulated it himself—"

"Wait a minute, Jake," Hawker said, interrupting. "This is the guy you want me to stop? It sounds like we ought to join him, if you ask me."

"Up to this point I think you're right, James," Hayes said

calmly, tapping his pipe into an ashtray. "I agree. Much of what Curtis has done is admirable. But in the last two years he has changed, changed drastically. Back in Atlanta he was known as a fine man, a decent man, a humanitarian man. Politically he is ultra–right wing, but even his adversaries on the left admired him for his honesty and sense of fair play. But three years ago Wellington Curtis decided that sending money and mercenaries to Masagua wasn't enough. He decided that in order to really contribute he would have to go there, himself. He decided he would appoint himself general of his little army and take full control of the rebel movement. Apparently he did rather well during the first year there. Brilliant historians aren't always brilliant military leaders in the field. But he was. He and his men fought bravely and honorably, and he made the Moscow-backed regulars of Masagua look foolish more than once. But then something happened. I don't know what. Maybe a year in the jungle fighting for survival is a little too much for someone from a cultured background to stand. At any rate Curtis's methods began to change. And his ideas, his . . . philosophies became unsound. In Masagua gruesome stories of his troops beheading babies, torturing women, and raping little boys and girls began to filter out of the jungle. Rather than refuting the news stories, Curtis cut down on his contact with the outside world. He refused to do any more interviews and warned that any journalists found within his camp would be executed on sight."

"You can't really blame him for that," Hawker said wryly.

Hayes smiled and continued. "Even so, a photograph of Colonel Curtis appeared in *Time* magazine two months ago. I don't know how it was smuggled out, but it was a startling photograph to see, if one had known Curtis before he left Atlanta—and I did. The photo showed Curtis, who is now in his early fifties, wearing nothing but a breechcloth, a gun belt, and camouflage paint. In his left hand he was holding the severed head of a small girl. In his right hand was a knife." Hayes took a sip of his mango juice, then returned it to the table. "James, in my opinion Colonel Wellington Curtis has gone quite insane."

Hawker thought for a moment. "I have no ill will for the people of Masagua, Jake, but what does your story have to do with you or me or Thy? Didn't we agree when we started as . . . partners that there was more than enough corruption in the United States to take care of? So far every one of our operations has taken place back home. Are you sure you want me to get involved in Central America?"

Hayes shook his head. "I'm quite sure I don't want you to get involved in the problems of Central America, James. Unfortunately Colonel Curtis's unsound methods are not just being used in Masagua. They are being used in the United States, too—Georgia, to be specific. I'll explain.

"When Curtis first got involved with the rebel cause in Masagua, he drew on his personal wealth to finance his operation, but to a greater extent he drew on the wealth of friends who agreed with his political views. When these weird rumors about him began appearing in the news, his friends were curious, but they were sure that Curtis would return and refute the stories. But Curtis didn't return. Instead he withdrew. He has spent the last two years in the jungle without making any public contact with his friends in the United States.

"Finally his friends got together and sent out an appeal for Curtis to return to the United States and set the record straight. His reply—sent through two aides—was so obscene, so offensive to his friends, and so strongly worded that the news media couldn't even use it. His friends abandoned him, leaving Curtis without sufficient funds to continue. So Curtis has devised a new way to solicit funds.

"One year ago he sent his two most trusted mercenaries, Shawn Pendleton and Greg Warren, back to the United States. Pendleton and Warren go by the ranks of captain in Colonel Curtis's little army, but they are really nothing more than hired thugs. They belonged to the Hell's Angels for a while and smuggled drugs; each was arrested for armed robbery and assault in the early seventies, but the charges were dropped on a technicality. These are the men Curtis is using to solicit funds for the rebel cause. And the way they solicit funds is not pretty. They have put together two squads of men. With those men they tour Georgia. At first they simply described the colonel's cause and asked for donations. But the money didn't come fast enough, so Curtis had them revise their methods. The two hit squads—and that's what they are—began to use brutal methods to get money. Blackmail, extortion, terrorism, and, in last three instances, murder. They are absolute fanatics, and they will stop at nothing." Hayes finished his fruit juice as Thy Estes, the beautiful redheaded United States senator reached out and took Hawker's hand.

"They've done terrible things, James," she said. "I know you admire what Curtis has done in Central America, but he's gotten way out of hand. There is no official way to stop him.

In Georgia the people are so terrified of his hit squads that they refuse to testify. And, of course, in Masagua we have no influence at all. Will you help? Will you go to Atlanta and try to infiltrate one of the two terrorist groups and put a stop to their bloody work?"

Hawker shrugged. "Have you forgotten, senator? The CIA wants my head on a platter. They have already come damn close to catching me twice." Hawker gave the woman a look that only she would understand. "In fact, I seem to remember spending a long cold night in a barn outside of Belfast, hiding from two of their agents. Don't you?"

Her smile had a glint of wickedness in it. "I don't remember it being *that* cold, Mr. Hawker—but that's not the point."

"Oh?"

"That's right, dear. The point is, I spoke with a Mr. Rehfuss of the Central Intelligence Agency—"

"You talked to Jerry?" Hawker said, leaning forward.

"Yes—at his request, by the way. And it seems that the CIA would like to enlist your help in cleaning up this Wellington Curtis business. As I said, the United States government has no influence in Masagua—"

"That never stopped the CIA before," Hawker put in.

"You may be right, but in this instance, with the news media doing everything in its power to cripple the president's Central American initiative, the Agency would rather keep a very low profile. Mr. Rehfuss said that they were interested in hiring someone to work free-lance. They would like to hire you again, Hawk."

"And drop all charges—whatever in hell the charges were?"

"If you agree to follow their orders"—the woman smiled—"for once."

"And the Agency wants me to go to Masagua and eliminate Curtis?"

"The Agency might," Hayes put in, "but we don't. I'm saying that as a friend, Hawk. It would be far too dangerous for you to go knocking around in Central America. But I think you could clear up the problems Curtis is causing in Georgia. That's the way to really get to him. That's the way to stop him. Shut off his money supply."

Hawker thought for a long moment before looking at his old friend. "Jake, I'm anxious as hell to get away from this jet-set life I've been living. But I can't just fly off to Georgia. Not just like that. From what I've heard about Curtis he deserves better. He may have gone insane—but the rumors also may have been started by bullshit journalists. And even if he did stray off the path, maybe it's not too late for someone to bring him back. Maybe someone can straighten him out. You said yourself that he had been doing good work in Masagua. And, frankly, I believe too strongly in his cause to just turn him off like a spigot. I think Wellington Curtis deserves another chance, Jake. He needs to be shown where he has gone wrong."

Hayes leaned forward, slightly impatient. "And how in the world do you propose to do that, James? Hack your way through the jungle, smile at his guards, wave at his Head-hunter Corps, sit down at his feet, and calmly explain to this madman why you are going to have to destroy his American organization if he doesn't get back on track?"

James Hawker stood up, chuckling. "If you'll set up the meeting for me, Jake, that's exactly what I propose to do . . ."

So Jake Hayes had arranged the meeting; a meeting with Curtis in Belize at eight P.M. at the Fort George Hotel on a Tuesday in June. But Curtis had sent his whore and confidante, Laurene Catocamez, instead. Now the woman had proposed taking him to Guatemala in the morning. By taking his key had she also proposed something more?

It would be a while before Hawker would find out. He exited the hotel to the walkway that led to his room. It was a clear Caribbean dusk: high, bright sliver of moon; orange afterglow of the setting sun; and a balmy wind that smelled of the sea. The Fort George Hotel was well named. Steel fence and barbed wire surrounded the grounds, protecting the outside entrances to the rooms. This was a more accurate picture of paradise in Belize and also of tropical retreats like Jamaica and the Bahamas; tourists had to be fenced away from the citizenry to protect them from the poverty and the crime and the hatred.

Hawker was anxious to get the hell away.

As he approached the door to his ground-floor room a rustling in the bushes drew his attention, a noise from behind. Hawker whirled quickly, reaching for the 9-mm. Beretta holstered beneath the sea-blue worsted blazer that he wore. But he was too late. Standing before him was the huge bearded black man he had seen moments earlier in the bar.

In the man's hand was a long-barreled revolver, pointed at Hawker's face . . .

THREE

"Your name is Hawker? James Hawker?" the big man demanded, walking slowly toward the vigilante. "Answer me!"

Hawker took a deep breath, trying to control the rush of adrenaline charging through him. "I have a policy against making sparkling conversation when someone is holding a gun on me."

The big man stopped and gave a deep, oily chuckle that was touched with the British accent of the islands. Hawker realized that the man reminded him of someone: Geoffrey Holder on the 7-Up commercials. "You are telling me you don't answer questions at the point of a gun?" The man smiled. "If that is true, Mr. Hawker, then I am very surprised that you are still alive."

"That makes two of us, friend. Now why don't you just put that weapon away before one of us gets hurt."

The man laughed again. "Yes, you are the James Hawker I have heard so much about. Calm in tight situations, they told me. Fearless—even taunting—when confronted by deadly force." The laugh turned into a sneer as the man took a quick step and slapped Hawker sharply across the face. "And do you know what my reply was, Mr. Hawker? I told them you have not yet met me. I told them that before I killed you—and I *will* kill you in a very few minutes—that I would have reduced you to tears, to begging for your life. I told them that I would have you on your knees."

His muscles tense, all his senses alert for the opening he needed, Hawker gave a mock sniffle as he wiped away the blood that now poured freely from his upper lip. "There," he said, "I'm in tears. Now I'm begging you: Put that weapon away, you fat fuck, before I stick it up your dirty black ass!"

Hawker got just the reaction he had hoped for. The big man's nostrils flared with anger, and Hawker drew back the revolver to club him with it. As he did, Hawker stepped down on the man's foot, knocked his gun hand away, and drove his fist deep into the man's solar plexus. The huge man gave a guttural *whoof*, bending over in agony, as the vigilante took the huge right arm in his hands and drove it across his knee. The big man let out a shriek as the revolver spun wildly into the air and landed with a clatter on the cement. Hawker reached for the Beretta, but before he could get to it, the black man gave a brutal kick that caught the vigilante on the inside of the thigh, just below and to the left of the scrotum. The force of the blow knocked him to the ground, and his attacker jumped on him.

Wheezing and grunting, the two men fought brutally to get a choke hold on the other's throat. The man was tremendously strong, and Hawker realized quickly that he would probably lose any life-and-death test of strength. But he also realized that what the man had in muscle, he lacked in brains. Hawker pretended for just a moment to be blacking out. Immediately the big man shifted his position so as to get a better grip. At that moment of vulnerability Hawker punched him hard in the throat, used his elbow to club the man's nose flat, then rolled away, reaching for his Beretta.

Realizing that the fight was lost, the black man jumped to his feet with startling speed and vaulted over the barbed-wire-topped fence, ripping his hands and shirt as he did.

Hawker did not shoot as the man disappeared into the darkness. After a few moments he holstered his weapon and began to take inventory of his own physical condition. His upper lip was still bleeding, his throat felt as if he had swallowed ground glass, and his inner thigh hurt like hell. "*Damn*," he whispered, breathing heavily. "What a night!"

The vigilante carried no handkerchief, so he used a small stick to pick up the man's weapon, careful not to smear whatever prints might be there. Who he could get to lift the prints—or who would even care that he was attacked—he did not know. Protecting the prints was an old cop habit, and he carried the weapon to the door of his hotel room and turned the knob.

It was locked. He had forgotten all about the woman, forgotten that she had left with his key.

Was the big black man her accomplice? Had she taken his key so that he would be left stranded on the walk outside, trying to get in?

Hawker gave the door a savage kick and called himself a foul name. How stupid could he be! A moment later, though, the door to his hotel room swung open. Laurene Catocamez stood looking at him. She wore one of Hawker's T-shirts. The darkness of her nipples stood out in contrast beneath the thin, white material. The shirt billowed out around the glistening swell of her lean hips and revealed the bottom curls of the triangle of her black pubic hair. She leaned against the door seal, a wry, sleepy, bedroom expression on her petulant lips. "Did I hear you call yourself a dumb fuck?" she asked, purring. "From what I have heard, James, dear, you are anything but . . ."

The woman stood there looking catlike, extremely desirable, but then her eyes seemed to focus and her expression changed suddenly to one of shock. "James, you've been hurt! My God, what happened to you?"

Hawker realized that he must look like a bloody mess. He shrugged off the woman's efforts to help him and limped past her to the bathroom. He plugged the sink, ran cold water, and dumped in a bucket of ice from the counter. He buried his right fist in the water, then submerged his face until the pain was too much to stand.

"Hand me a towel, damn it," he sputtered.

The woman found a towel and began to dab at his face. "Why are you so mad at me? Please, tell me what happened!"

Hawker jerked the towel from her and finished drying his face. "What happened, dear lady, is that the man you had posted outside my room failed. He tried to kill me, tried very damn hard, but tonight just wasn't his night. He left with what I truly hope is a fractured arm"—Hawker motioned to the revolver on the counter—"and without his gun." Hawker tossed the towel away and glared at the woman. "Now, you can make it very easy on yourself, Laurene, by telling me all about it. Or, if you like, I can make you talk. And don't think for an instant that the fact that you are very obviously a woman bothers me."

The woman's pale mahogany face turned a slow, deep shade of oiled wood. Anger. Outrage. She whirled away from Hawker, yanked one of his jackets off the hanger, and covered herself. "There! Is that better? You really know how to put a woman out of the mood!"

Hawker couldn't believe what he was hearing. "*Me*? Wellington Curtis tries to have me killed on my first night in Belize and you expect me to come in here, jump into bed with you, tell you any little secrets I might be hiding, and then act as happy as a lark? Come on, lady. I don't know what jungle you crawled out of, but people aren't quite so naive in the real world—"

"Why would Colonel Curtis have you killed?" she shouted, interrupting, her fists planted on her hips. "He honestly hopes you have come to help him!"

"Then who in the hell was that guy waiting for me outside? He knew my name; he knew all about me. He wasn't just one of your run-of-the-mill drugged-out island thieves. He was a pro. A dumb pro, but a pro just the same."

"James, I told you that I am Wellington Curtis's confidante, and I am. So I won't pretend not to know something of your past. Any number of people could have arranged to have that man waiting for you. But my guess is that it was the CIA— aren't they after you too?"

"It couldn't be the CIA because—" Hawker stopped himself in mid-sentence, realizing that he was about to give away some important information. After a moment he looked at the woman. "Get out," he said. "Now."

"But my clothes . . . I'm not even dressed!"

Hawker had taken her by the arm and was leading her to the door. "I'll call the front desk and have them send a maid with a key to your room—"

"I don't have a room!"

"You will when I get off the phone to the front desk."

Hawker locked the door against the woman's protestations. He opened one of the Belikin beers he had been keeping in the now empty ice bucket and drank half of it in a gulp as he sat by the phone. First he arranged for another room and then got through to the overseas operator. "That's right, Operator," he said, almost yelling into the phone, "Jerry Rehfuss, Washington, D.C." He gave her the private telephone number of his former CIA connection, hung up the phone, and waited.

Hawker was soaking his hand in ice water when the phone rang ten minutes later.

The voice at the other end sounded cautious, reluctant to talk, and a million miles away. "James? James Hawker? Is that really you?"

"It's me, Jer. Alive and well—no thanks to you."

"Ah, James, a public phone line may not be the place to discuss our business—"

"You keep a voltage meter on your end, Jer. You tell *me*: Should we discuss our business?"

"Well, no, probably not. But it depends, James—"

"Someone tried to exercise a contract on me tonight, Jerry," Hawker said, cutting in. "He gave it a good try, but he fell a little short."

Rehfuss's voice became even more cautious, and Hawker guessed that there was either someone in the room with him or the line, indeed, was being tapped. "I'm not surprised that they failed, James. You're a good businessman. Tell me, what did this person look like?"

"A big black guy with a beard. The beard might have been fake. He had an island accent, a deep voice. He knew too much about me. It sounds like one of your free-lancers to me. It's a shame, too, Jer, because I had heard that our companies were going to be friends again. I was looking forward to the negotiations."

"You said it was a large black man, James?" Rehfuss asked, pressing on. "Please be more exact in your description. And you haven't even told me where you're calling from."

"You don't really expect me to tell you after what happened tonight, do you, Jer?"

"How can I help, James, if you won't trust me?"

"You can help by telling me if your representatives still have orders to exercise that contract. I have his equipment, by the way, and his prints, too, I assume—not that anyone really gives a damn."

There was a long silence on the Washington end, and Hawker knew that Rehfuss was talking to someone else. He wondered who. Finally the lanky CIA agent came back to the phone. "I hate to admit it, James, but it could be one of our representatives. Orders went out last week that we were going to deal with you on a more friendly basis—temporarily, at least. We were waiting until we closed the deal with you, and apparently not all the orders got through."

"Well, Jer, old buddy, tell your buddies at the head office that I will be a lot more amenable to a deal if your sales reps aren't trying to cut my throat."

"Right away, James—but please do this for me: Promise you'll get back within the next three days. We need to discuss—"

"I'll be in touch, Jer. I'll be in touch."

Hawker hung up the phone and sat moodily finishing his beer. *To hell with it*, he thought. *To hell with them all. I work best when I work on my own. If Laurene Catocamez—or whatever her name is—still wants to take me to Curtis, I'll go. But I'll trust no one. And if it looks like Curtis needs a kick in the ass, I'll do it my way, in Masagua or Atlanta or wherever I decide.*

Hawker stripped off his torn and bloody clothes, turned on the shower as hot as he could stand it, and tried to suds one of the all-time shitty days away. When he was finished, he slid the Beretta under his pillow and crawled beneath the sheets.

A few minutes later, just as he was dozing off, there came a light tapping at the door. Hawker was on his feet in an instant, the weapon cool in his big right hand. "Who is it?"

The tumbler of the lock clicked, and the door swung open. Laurene Catocamez stood in the doorway wearing a long, sheer negligee instead of the T-shirt. "I'm sorry, James," she whispered. "That's what I came to tell you. Please believe that we had nothing to do with it. Let's be friends."

Hawker switched the Beretta to his left hand and walked naked to the door. He could feel the woman's eyes on him. He pulled the door wider and said coldly, "If you want to fuck, let's cut out all the bullshit and just fuck. But if you've come looking for more information, don't waste your time, lady. I have too many friends as it is. I don't need any more."

Laurene Catocamez stepped into the room. Hawker noticed that she was shivering slightly. She wrapped her arms around him and rubbed her face against his chest. "Then we have something in common, James, dear," she said. "Neither of us wants to be friends, but we both have something the other wants . . ."

FOUR

Belize International Airport seemed a pompous name for the concrete runway and drab terminal with its broken windows and walls scribbled with graffiti. As bored tourists waited in line to be ticketed, Laurene Catocamez led Hawker through the terminal outside to a twin-engine Trislander.

Hawker looked at the plane. "We're flying?"

The woman had opened the bottom door to the aft luggage compartment. "Yes. Part of the way. We will then go by jeep, and then horseback."

Hawker, who had ridden horses while on a mission in Texas, winced. He didn't like horses. "I can't wait," he said.

"We should be there in about four hours."

"This is a lunch flight, right? Where's the stewardess? Where's the pilot?"

The woman slammed the luggage compartment and opened the door to the cockpit. "There is no stewardess, and I'm the pilot," she said, not smiling as Hawker winced again.

As the plane lifted off, the clutter and slums of Belize City fell behind, replaced by coconut palms, black rivers, and jungle. Ahead were craggy, low mountains covered in waxy green. Hawker sat quietly as the woman, wearing headphones, concentrated on flying. Below, the dirt roads gradually narrowed, then were swallowed up by the tropical gloom of rain forest. Flocks of white birds bloomed from the trees and took flight. Steam lifted off the rivers in a pale haze. In the forest were sporadic clearings that held wooden shacks, tiny fields, dugout canoes on creek banks. As the plane passed overhead, men looked up from their work in pale golden banana patches. Children ran naked in the yards, waving.

"A poor country," said the woman.

"A poor country," Hawker agreed.

Since they had awoken together that morning the woman had given no touch of affection, said no words of endearment. For that Hawker was glad. He had taken what he wanted from her, just as she had taken from him. It was a pleasant, physical thing but edged with a weird undertone of violence. They had made sex, not love. That night she had stepped into his room, locked the door behind her, then stripped off the negligee in one feverish motion.

"No more words," she had whispered, taking Hawker, naked, into her small, strong hands. "No more words. Just fuck me; fuck me any way you wish, as hard as you wish, as long as you wish. I will do anything you ask. Take me now."

The fine, Latin delicacy of her face did not match the peasant contours of her body. Her breasts were sharp cones with dark, elongated nipples that, when stroked or touched with his tongue, made the woman groan feverishly, as if about to orgasm from mere touch. Her hips were strong and wide, made for breeding and birthing, and when Hawker entered her, she spread her legs wider and wider, as if she wanted everything, all parts of the man, inside her. At the end of their first frenzied joining the woman had writhed, then screamed out loud, as if in ecstatic pain as she orgasmed.

"That was wonderful!"

Hawker, sweating, had smiled. "Quite a workout, complete with a cheerleader."

Up on one elbow, she touched her finger between her legs, then touched the same finger to her tongue. "You taste so good."

"I wouldn't know."

"I would like a better taste."

"You may have to give me a minute or two."

"I will give you one minute. Only one." The woman kissed his chest, his abdomen, slid down him, and locked her arms around his thighs. "While I wait do you mind if I do this?"

With her left hand she directed him into her mouth, tracing the underside of his penis with her tongue, then sucked, hard.

Hawker shuddered. "Maybe half a minute. Maybe that's all I need."

The woman lifted her head. "Do you love me, James? Just a little?"

"No. You know I don't."

"You are a cruel bastard," she said with an evil smile. "Would such a tiny lie hurt you?"

"Our thirty seconds are up, woman. Get back to work."

She had opened her mouth wide, her eyes watching his face as she took him into her. She began gently, like a young girl with a Popsicle, but gradually she became more and more demanding, sweating and writhing between his legs like a starved feral creature. At his moment of release he looked down briefly to see if she would turn away. She did not. Instead her eyes glistened with a sort of wild triumph as she gulped eagerly, hungrily, wanting more of him and more and more and more . . .

Now they rode together like two business acquaintances on a junket. Hawker was glad. They had given each other pleasure, nothing more. He hated clinging women who felt that after opening their legs to a man they were entitled to his loyalties and to his soul. The woman clearly expected nothing more, and he admired her cold acceptance of their relationship.

"Look," she said, pointing ahead and to port. "Do you see?"

It took Hawker a moment to find what she meant. Below, protruding above the distant canopy of green, was a massive pyramid. The ancients had built it on a mountaintop, built it of gray stone on a cliff that dominated all the valleys below, like a pale altar in a sanctuary of jungle green.

"That is the temple of Xunantunich," she said. "The Mayans built it more than a thousand years ago. They were a great people, a great race. See how the temple dominates the jungle; jungle in every direction as far as the eye can see—even from two thousand feet. The Mayans built a great civilization out of the jungle, but they could not conquer the diseases of the Spaniard."

Hawker wasn't prepared for the bitterness in her voice. He

said, "I'm surprised a woman from Masagua knows so much about Belize."

"Belize? There is no Belize. It is an invention of its silly people. There is no Belize and no Guatemala and no Masagua, if you really care to know what I think. There are only the mountains and the jungle and the seas. This is the land of the Mayans. Since the arrival of the Spaniards every conqueror has been a thief, a tourist on this soil. This land will always belong to the people who built that temple."

"You talk like you hate the Spanish, but you are obviously Spanish."

"If one is raped at birth, is not one still a virgin at heart? In my heart, I am Mayan—as are most of the people of Masagua. I know that I have Spanish blood, but I hate it. It is the blood of the thief. There is also the blood of the Negro in me, but I despise that too. It is the blood of the eternal child, the slave's blood." She looked at him from the corner of her eye. "Do you wonder that I take pride in being Mayan? Is your blood so pure that you don't understand?"

"Nothing pure about my blood," Hawker said wryly. "I just had no idea that you were Mayan—or that you even cared. I thought this whole thing was because you hate communists."

"I do hate them. All of us, all of us in the cause hate the communists. They are robots; they are machines who do not think. We must defeat them; we must kill them all. But in the end our goal is to recapture our land, to return our country and all the other countries of Central America to their rightful owners. To the Mayans."

Hawker noticed how white the woman's hands had become

on the wheel of the plane. He said, "I've never met Colonel Wellington Curtis, but I'm pretty sure he's no Indian."

"That is a problem that will be resolved in the future," she said simply. "He understands that too. For now he is happy. For now we need him."

Hawker began to watch for more Mayan temples in the jungle. He saw a few that, like Xunantunich, stood bare above the haze of green. More often, though, the temples he saw were pyramid shapes beneath clinging vines and furious growth of the tropics; centers of ancient civilizations that archaeologists had not yet uncovered.

The woman, he noticed, had grown suddenly anxious. Her eyes darted from side to side, reminding him of a nervous Sunday driver. She lifted the half wheel of the controls, and the plane began a sharp descent. Just above the gigantic trees, it seemed, she leveled off. For the first time Hawker perceived the speed at which they were traveling as the jungle, at low altitude, rolled by.

"See an interesting bird?" Hawker asked chidingly.

"In a way," she said. "In a way."

At that moment there was a blur of khaki outside his window and an explosion of noise so unexpected that Hawker ducked away. "Holy shit! What was that?"

The woman didn't answer. Ahead the blur slowed, turned, seemed to hover directly above the treetops, facing them. It was a fighter jet painted camouflage green. The jet was so close that Hawker could now see the toy figure of the pilot. "How does he do that? He's not moving. That's not some kind of helicopter, is it?"

"It's a Harrier, a British fighter. It can stop in midair and land like a helicopter, but it's all jet."

"The way he's stopped like that, it's like he's waiting on us."

"He is."

From the radio transceiver came: "*Securitade, securitade*; warning to twin-engine Trislander, registry unknown. You are about to leave British-controlled airspace of Belize for airspace of Guatemala. Guatemalan airspace is forbidden to aircraft without proper authorization. Do you copy?"

Into the hand mike the woman replied, "This is Trislander zero-niner-five-niner-niner. We copy. We are a missionary craft of international registry. We are entering Guatemalan airspace unarmed, carrying foodstuff and medicine for the Christian Indians. We will report our intent at Guatemala City."

There was a touch of resignation in the British pilot's voice. "Twin-engine Trislander of international registry, have I made my warning clear? You are about to enter Guatemalan airspace. Please acknowledge."

"Affirmative. We acknowledge."

"Good luck to you, then, ma'am," the voice on the radio replied, and the Harrier lifted suddenly, banked to port, and disappeared with a jet thrust that rocked the twin-engine plane.

"You handled that well," said Hawker.

"I handle many things well, James. Please don't sound so surprised. I have been on my own since I was thirteen years old. My mother died of black-water fever, and I never knew my father. Resourcefulness for most people is something to be exercised on a whim, like a game. But for someone like me it has always been the difference between success and failure, sometimes life and death." She glanced at him to make sure he was listening. "Does it bother you to have your life depend on the resourcefulness of a woman? Are you that kind of man? Your life does depend on me, you know. In a few minutes I must fly this plane through a series of narrow mountain passes. If there is low cloud cover, I will have to fly by memory only. Not only that, but we must land in a clearing that has no markings of any kind. I must find it, make sure that the government forces of Masagua aren't waiting in ambush, then land on a field considered far too short for this plane. So you see? Your life does depend on me. Does that make you nervous?"

Hawker stifled a mock yawn. "I'm terrified," he said. "Hurry up and find that airfield, lady. I have to take a wizz."

"A wizz?"

"Yes. A wizz is something of mine that even you can't control, Laurene, dear. I hope . . ."

FIVE

The plane twisted and turned through the narrow mountain passes of Guatemala. Sheer green jungle walls plunged toward them, dipped away, and disappeared, one after another.

"You can fly this route by memory?" Hawker asked casually, trying to relax in his seat.

"I didn't say that," the woman said, managing a smile as she concentrated on the next abrupt turn. "I said that if it was cloudy, I would have to try."

"I'm glad it's not cloudy," Hawker said.

"Yes, me too. But the day will come when it will be cloudy. And then I will have to discover just how good my memory is." The woman pulled back on the wheel, and the plane climbed desperately, narrowly missing a craggy wall of jungle.

Then they were out of the passes, and Hawker could see a fast clear river below, rushing through the lush tropical growth. The land was wild with bright flowers, gigantic mahogany and Guanacaste trees, waterfalls.

"It looks like paradise," said Hawker.

"It is paradise, James. On the south side of the river is Masagua, my country. Our army has been training on the north side of the river to avoid the government troops."

"And how does the government of Guatemala feel about that?"

"I doubt if the government of Guatemala even knows that this valley exists. Very few know of it. That is why Colonel Curtis has chosen it for our training grounds. Like all Americans, you are surprised that places of beauty still exist in the world unknown to men and governments and builders. I find it comforting that in my country more is unknown than known." The woman tapped the throttle and the plane decreased speed. "Hold on; the field—see it? That clearing. I'm going to circle once before landing. Please keep your eye open for soldiers."

"Laurene, you've got to be kidding. An entire division could hide in that jungle without being seen."

The woman reached back, picked up and threw a canvas covering on the floor. What had been beneath the canvas were several automatic weapons, a crate of ammunition, and a box of grenades. "I am not kidding—please look for soldiers. But, if they are there, we are ready. Okay?"

Hawker picked up one of the automatics. It was one of the early-model Uzi submachine guns. Its wooden stock made it stern-heavy, awkward. He slid in a full clip of 9-mm. parabellum cartridges. "Because I have no choice," he said, "I'm ready."

The woman dropped the plane lower, circling. "I see a jeep in the trees," Hawker said. "There's a man standing beside it. He's wearing a wide-brimmed hat."

"Yes," said the woman. "That will be Mario. He has come to pick us up. Do you see anything else?"

"Trees; just a lot of trees—hey, and there's something . . . something climbing through the trees like crazy."

The woman banked lower. She laughed. "Monkeys. They are frightened by the plane. See how they rush to escape to the highest branches?"

Hawker did not smile. "Right. The highest branches." Hawker checked the safety tang of the old Uzi. Full automatic was two notches forward of safety.

The woman nosed the plane down easily, dropping it over the trees into the wind, touching the wheels onto the rough grass as the carriage of the plane creaked and rattled like an old car. She brought the plane to a stop at the end of the short runway as Mario, the tiny man in the wide hat, came driving out to meet them in a red Toyota Land Cruiser with no top.

"We'll unload the luggage and weapons, then tie down the plane and cover it with a camouflaged netting," the woman said as they jumped down to the ground. "We have about a twenty-mile ride before we meet the horses."

"Wellington Curtis will meet us there?"

"Colonel Curtis is with the troops. He never leaves them."

"After that plane ride I don't blame him."

Carrying the Uzi, Hawker grabbed his duffel. While the woman threw out her baggage and supplies Hawker kept his eye on the line of trees. He had never seen such huge trees—even in Venezuela. The trees were ancient, massive, black. Steam seemed to rise from the trees, and the elephant-ear-size leaves sagged in the stillness and heat. The air was gaseous with the smell of vegetation, rot, black earth. In the distance there were the screams of birds and the chattering of monkeys. The sounds, the humid smell of jungle, the stillness, all touched some prehistoric nerve in Hawker, some chord he recognized but could not identify. He could feel the chord deep within him, a dark thing with catlike eyes and teeth of the carnivore, the chord of the beast. In that startling moment Hawker felt as if he should rip his clothes away, grab the woman by the hair, run her naked into the jungle to hunt, to rear offspring, to survive.

"James? Are you all right?"

"What? Oh, yeah, sure. I was just listening to the monkeys. They make quite a racket." In his mind he reminded himself: Why would monkeys frightened by a plane escape to the highest limbs of the trees? "And I was just watching the line of trees," he said. "You said to watch, didn't you?"

"Have you seen something?"

"No. Not yet."

"Not yet?"

"Not yet."

Hawker and the woman helped the little man, Mario, load the supplies into the Land Cruiser. The woman kept up a rattling dialogue in Spanish. Hawker's Spanish was fair, but he had to concentrate if he wanted to understand. Now, though, he was concentrating on something else.

When the Toyota was loaded, the camouflage netting staked down, Mario slid in behind the wheel, Laurene Catocamez took the passenger seat, and Hawker sat on the luggage, one hand on the roll bar, the other resting the little submachine gun against the side of his head. As they started out across the field toward the jungle, Hawker quietly opened the top of one of the crates. Six grenades sat within, like metal eggs in compartments.

He put two of the grenades at his feet and squatted down, waiting. If he was wrong, it would do no harm. If he was right, he wanted to be ready.

Unfortunately he was right.

The soldiers opened fire way too soon, when the Land Cruiser was two hundred meters from the line of trees. The first hail of fire slapped through the grass with a scything sound followed by the muted *poppa-pop* of the weapons.

Behind them the plane exploded in bright orange flames and black smoke.

Something hot splattered across Hawker's face as Mario, the driver, slumped sideways. The Land Cruiser veered wildly and the woman screamed. Hawker jumped into the front of the vehicle and saw, in a look, that the driver was dead. He rolled the corpse out into the grass, and grabbed the wheel, and turned sharply away from the fire.

"Get down!" Hawker yelled, shoving the woman roughly to the floor.

He began to drive a serpentine route across the field, gradually angling toward what appeared to be an opening in the forest. Slugs *ping-tinged* off the body of the vehicle, and Hawker knew that at any moment the Toyota could explode into flames.

"Who are they?" Hawker demanded.

The woman was in hysterics. "My God, they shot poor Mario! Why did you leave him? Answer me, damn it! Answer me!"

"Because he was dead! Who are those soldiers?"

"Oh, Mario. Poor, poor Mario . . ."

Just ahead, fifty meters away behind some bushes, Hawker saw movement. He stood, his foot still on the accelerator, and opened fire. On full automatic, the Uzi shredded the bushes. One man in army khaki jumped to his feet, clawing at the black holes where his eyes once were. Two others tumbled out, their chests oozing red gore. Other men, he saw, climbed farther into the underbrush.

Hawker shoved the Uzi at the woman. "Stick a new clip in this. Did you hear me?! Reload this or we're all going to die!"

As the Land Cruiser careened past the dead soldiers Hawker pulled the pins of two grenades and tossed the grenades into the brush. They exploded behind the Toyota, and in the mirror Hawker saw two men stagger drunkenly into the clearing. The blast had sheared off one of the men's arms, and the stump that remained spurted blood.

"Is it reloaded yet?" Hawker demanded.

The woman thrust the Uzi at him. Her eyes were glazed with shock and rage. "Yes, damn it! But I want you to know right now that I hold you responsible for the loss of Mario!"

"He was dead, damn it!"

"Do you know that for sure? Are you a doctor? At least we could have carried him with us and given him a proper burial!"

"Christ, you act like he was your brother or something."

"He *was*, you bastard. He was . . ."

SIX

The next five minutes seemed like five hours.

The vigilante carried on a running gun-battle with soldiers. More than once he thought of abandoning the vehicle and the woman and striking out into the jungle alone.

Instead he clung stubbornly to the wheel with his left hand while holding the Uzi in his right.

What had looked to be an opening in the forest was really nothing more than a muddy logging path. The Land Cruiser roared down it, jumping and jolting through the potholes. Once they drove into what appeared to be a wide puddle. The puddle was so deep that water came up over the floorboards, yet the Land Cruiser continued to run.

Ahead, someone had dragged a tree across the trail. In the bushes on either side Hawker could see men waiting. He slid down into the seat, touched the brake, and made ready to shift into reverse. But in the rearview mirror he could see more soldiers running after them.

"Grab one of the automatics and put down some fire behind us," Hawker ordered.

The woman wiped her eyes defiantly, but she took up a weapon, slid in a fresh clip, and began to fire. She fired tentatively at first. But then her anger took control, and she began to spray her little Uzi back and forth passionately, a look of sheer hatred on her face.

"You sons of whores!" she screamed, sobbing as she fired. "You cowards!"

Behind them, soldiers tumbled to the ground or dived for the trees, but there were still too many of them. Hawker realized that somehow he would have to get past the fallen tree and the soldiers, who waited in ambush ahead.

The vigilante jammed the Land Cruiser into four-wheel-drive low, then upshifted into second, gaining speed.

"Hold on!" he yelled. "Reload and get ready to fire ahead of us."

Hawker sat crouched behind the wheel, headed straight for the fallen tree. Then, at the last moment, he swung the wheel to the left just as the soldiers stood to open fire. He could see the looks on their faces clearly as the red vehicle bore down on them, could see their eyes grow wide as they realized that the Toyota was going to run them down.

The first soldier they hit flew up onto the hood of the jeep, a glazed look in his eyes. Hawker tipped his submachine gun over the windshield and squeezed off a quick burst. The 9-mm. slugs knocked the soldier away, into the grass.

The woman was laying a sheet of heavy fire off to the right, and Hawker grabbed another grenade and tossed it overhand to his left.

Behind them was an explosion and more screams of agony.

Then, unexpectedly, there was silence, silence but for the roaring whine of the four-by-four as it strained against its gears. Silence but for the sobbing of the woman as she reached for still another fresh clip.

Hawker took her wrist. "It's okay," he said soothingly. "I think that's it. I think we've made it."

The woman tore her hand away and jammed in a fresh clip, anyway. "You do not know them!" she snapped. "They are not men, they are animals! Now that they have found us they will not give up. They will never stop!"

"Fine," he said, "just stay ready, then. But don't fire unless you need to. The sound of a weapon carries a lot farther than the sound of this jeep."

"Bastards!" she shouted at the trees.

Hawker turned his concentration to driving, dodging potholes, taking the best route through the gloom of the rain forest. He drove silently for many minutes before the woman beside him sighed, then settled back into the seat. She lit a cigarette with shaking hands.

"I'm sorry about your brother," Hawker said softly. "If I had known, I wouldn't have shoved his body out. But he was dead. There's no doubt about that. But he was killed instantly. He probably didn't feel a thing. He didn't suffer."

It was so long before she responded that Hawker thought she hadn't heard him. "He suffered enough in his life," she said finally. "I'm glad he didn't suffer in death. The way I acted back there, I am sorry. It was my way of mourning for him. I will miss my little Mario, but he is dead now, and there is nothing I can do about it. He is gone."

"You didn't tell me you had a brother."

"There are many things I did not tell you about me. Mario was my youngest brother. There was a sister too. I raised them both, from the time I was thirteen when we were left alone. I was, in many ways, their mother. It was very difficult for all of us. We were much too young to be on our own."

"Your sister? Is she . . . still with you?"

Laurene Catacomez shrugged. "I do not know. When she was fourteen, I was sixteen. A man from Guatemala City came to our village. He was very fat, very rich. He had a gold tooth. My sister was very beautiful with the body of a woman despite her age. He took her away. He said he wanted her to be his wife, but I felt he took her away to sell her on the street. I told her this, but she would not listen. She was a dreamy thing, our little Limona. She liked pretty dresses and bright ribbons. The man promised her an automobile. Nothing could stop her from going. So then it was just Mario and I. He was a good brother, and when I became interested in the rebel cause, he followed along, not because he believed in the cause but because he did not want to be alone. He had not the heart for fighting, so Colonel Curtis allowed him to do the cooking and other chores for the camp. I felt sure that I would die by violence before my dear Mario."

"Laurene, the soldiers who attacked us, were they Guatemalan?"

"No. I do not think so. I am sure they were government forces from Masagua."

"Yet they crossed the river into Guatemala? Weren't they taking a serious risk?"

The woman's laugh was sarcastic. "The borders are not so well drawn in Central America, nor are they so well respected. The government forces live only to kill. It does not matter to them where they kill."

"Then they must know where your rebel army trains. If that's true, doesn't it seem reasonable to expect them to attack as soon as they regroup?"

"Yes," she said, "it does seem reasonable." Looking at Hawker, she added, "My poor Americano. You came here for a brief meeting, yet you have landed in the middle of a war. Let us hope you get out alive."

"Let us hope," James Hawker said, parroting her.

The horses were waiting where Laurene's brother had tied them, five splay-legged animals that slumped beneath the hornless saddles like vultures.

Hawker finally found time to urinate, then he and the woman strapped the gear on the two packhorses, hid the Toyota as best as they could, then set off along the river through the rain forest.

The vigilante put a grenade in one of the oversized pockets of his Egyptian cotton safari shirt and slung the old Uzi across his back. After a few miles of riding through the pale gloom of the forest, the woman led them up a steep gorge into the foothills, away from the river.

"We don't have far to go now," she said, stopping her horse momentarily at a broad tree with black-green leaves. From the tree she twisted off several avocado pears and tossed one to Hawker. "Colonel Curtis asked that I blindfold you before taking you on this trail. After what we have been through, though, I don't think it's necessary. But before we go into camp, I'll have to blindfold you for appearance's sake. I hope you don't mind."

From a smaller tree Hawker took a handful of tiny green limes. He squirted lime juice onto the avocado and ate. "And what if I choose not to be blindfolded at all?"

The woman shrugged. "I would prefer that you did refuse. That way you would never be allowed to leave us." The woman kicked her horse and left Hawker sitting there, unsure about whether to feel flattered or angry.

The narrow trail climbed higher and higher into the mountains. There was a whoof of distant thunder, and the leaves in the high trees began to rattle. Hawker realized that it was raining, a warm rain that plastered the shirt to the woman's sharp breasts. The vigilante felt a stir of strong physical wanting, and he wondered what it was that attracted him so to the woman. Perhaps it's her anger, he thought. It makes her indifferent to the past and to the future. She seems to accept everything for exactly what it is: hardship, killing, sex, she takes them all at face value. She lives in the present, in the instant of her breathing, and that makes her a damn unusual woman.

"There," she said, pointing. "Do you see?"

In the near distance a small river leapt off the brink of a cliff forming a waterfall. The waterfall glistened and roared in the gray light of the storm, disappearing into the bright flowers of the jungle.

"Yeah," said Hawker. "It's very pretty."

"It's also our first checkpost. I must blindfold you now."

Hawker shrugged. "Okay, fine. But if you see anything the least bit suspicious, let me know immediately, damn it."

The woman maneuvered her horse beside his and tied a bright red bandanna over his face.

"Can you see?"

"Yeah. The inside of this bandanna."

Hawker was surprised to feel her lips claim his in a passionate, but brief, kiss. "What a strange sense of humor you have, James Hawker."

Hawker allowed himself to be led up the twisting trail like a child on a park pony. The roar of the waterfall drew nearer, and he heard the woman call out a greeting in Spanish that was returned by the voices of two men.

"This is the Americano?"

"*Si.* Colonel Curtis is in camp waiting?"

"Our colonel is in camp, but do you not think he will be jealous of this handsome gringo man-child?" one of the guards chided. "Perhaps he will insist that Ramon and I scar his pretty white face—"

"Silence," the woman cut in. "Are you so sure that this man does not speak Spanish—"

"I do not care what the gringo hears!"

"Save your nastiness, Balserio. The government forces approach. They attacked us after we landed. My brother, Mario, was murdered. This man beside me fought more bravely than you have ever fought. Stand aside so we may pass!"

They rode for only a short time before the woman brought

the horses to a stop again. There was an edge to her voice as she spoke, and it took Hawker a moment to recognize the edge as nervousness. He had not heard nervousness in her voice before.

"We are only a short way from the camp," she said. "I would like to prepare you."

"Don't tell me—you want to tie my hands, right?"

"I am not joking. You are a man of the world and have no doubt seen many . . . strange things. But it is possible that some things you see in this camp may appear stranger than they actually are. You are an outsider. You have come from a comfortable, modern world. Our world is not comfortable and it is not modern. Our war is not a modern war, though it is sometimes fought with modern weapons."

"What in the hell are you getting at, Laurene? I'm getting a little tired of sitting here with my eyes covered, listening to your Ping-Pong talk. If you have something to say, come out and say it."

"I am only asking that you do not judge Colonel Curtis—and his methods—too quickly. He is a brilliant man, but he has had to live in a strange world these last two years. The jungle does things to a man from your civilization. It changes all men, even him. I do not always approve of what he does, but he is much brighter than me, much brighter than you and all of us, and he has a reason for everything—"

"Laurene, damn it, tell me what you're trying to say, or I'm going to rip this blindfold off and go in and look for myself."

"Perhaps that is the best way," the woman said softly. "But, before you do, I want you to promise that you will not judge him too quickly. I have been as honest with you as I can be. Last night, James, we shared something that was very good. If you have any appreciation for what passed between us, then grant me this favor: Do not judge the colonel too quickly."

"Okay, okay," said Hawker. "I promise. Now let's get going."

SEVEN

Hawker took the woman's words of warning as an uncharacteristic insertion of the dramatic. What could he possibly see in the camp of the Masaguan rebel army that he hadn't seen at some other time in his life?

Hawker was wrong. There were a great many things he had yet to see. And the camp was one of them.

Around him he could hear voices, some speaking in low Spanish, others in guarded English. Someone called out for the colonel as the horses came to a rocking stop, blowing air. It was cool here, and Hawker could hear the sound of running water—a brook? But there was something else too: mixed with the sweet odor of jasmine and frangipani was an odd, rancid odor, like a mixture of sweat and animal grease. And there was a great stillness about the place, too, despite the voices, despite the clump of bare feet on soft earth—a strange, deathly stillness not related to sound.

"Can I take my blindfold off yet?" Hawker asked loudly, not sure where the woman was.

"By all means, Mr. James Hawker," said a man's articulate, enthusiastic voice. "Take off your blindfold and climb down off that poor horse. You've had a long journey and you must be very hungry."

Hawker stripped away the bandanna and blinked into the splotched light of a jungle clearing. Twenty or thirty men encircled him, spreading out from just behind the man who now held out his hand to Hawker. "I am Wellington Curtis, Mr. Hawker," the man said in his rich Southern accent. "We're damn glad to have you with us. I've been wanting to meet you for a long, long time."

Hawker slid off the horse and took the man's firm hand. For a moment he was speechless. This was not the Wellington Curtis he had expected. The Wellington Curtis of his imagination was the one he knew from the dust jackets of the two books on military history: a well-groomed Atlanta aristocrat with gray hair at the temples, wire-rimmed glasses, tweed suit, the stomach paunch of the scholar, and the wry, bemused expression of a middle-aged man who lived his adventures through his typewriter.

The Wellington Curtis of the dust jackets and the man who now stood before him were two very different people. This Wellington Curtis wore loose khaki pants belted tightly around a lean waist. His chest was broad, covered with matted gray hair, and his arms were long and corded as he rested one hand on a black-handled fighting knife and the other on his military-issue canteen. His face was gaunt beneath a three-day growth of beard, beaming expression, bushy gray eyebrows, and eyes that had a pale, wild look, like someone who had gone too long without food or water. Most striking of all, Curtis's head had been completely shaved, giving him a sinister, Oriental appearance, like a mad Buddhist monk. The broad, bald head glistened with sweat, and Curtis wiped a big hand over it, flinging the water away.

"You are hungry?" he repeated. "I have had my men butcher a mountain tapir to celebrate your arrival. Have you ever had tapir, Mr. Hawker? It's a strange-looking creature, like a cross between an elephant and a mule, but the meat is really damn good. Reminds me of my boyhood days in Georgia when we'd hunt wild hogs and barbecue a couple of tender sow haunches. Better than any pork you'll ever get back in the states. Unfortunately Laurene tells me that we have company below the mountain, so I'm going to have to ask you to take a snack instead, then we'll have a full meal later."

"You are going to attack them?"

The older man smiled. "In our own way, Mr. Hawker, in our own way."

Curtis turned. Immediately a path cleared for them through the crowd of people. Like Curtis, the men all wore khaki pants, side arms, canteens, and knives. Unlike Curtis, they all wore military-issue fatigue shirts with epaulets, name tags, and gaudy, subdued unit patches bearing a screaming red skull and crossbones. Hawker guessed that the uniforms Curtis had had custom-made for them and were like none he had ever seen, a cross between garish Italian and African white hunter. The men were a mixture of Hispanics and Americans in about a three-to-one ratio. The Hispanics were generally small, lean, intense men with wild, dark eyes and mustaches. The Americans were of the Southern rawboned variety: florid faces, thick necks, gaunt cheeks, sandy hair. Hawker found their presence strangely reassuring. Despite Hollywood's hackneyed view of the male Southerner as an overweight, tobacco-chewing sadist, Hawker knew that the South consistently produced some of the brightest politicians, scholars, and military leaders in America and, undoubtedly, some of the best athletes. If Curtis had gone insane, it seemed unlikely that he could continue to hold the respect of men such as this. Yet they obviously did respect him. Hawker was beginning to believe that his friend, Jake Hayes, and his lover, Senator Thy Estes, were both wrong about Curtis.

He would change his mind in a very short time.

He followed Curtis down a rocky path into a little jungle hollow where a whole village of substantial tree houses had been built high off the ground. Below them and to one side was a long open mess area with stone ovens and plank tables. Next to that was a neat little cottage made of raw clapboard. It had a porch and mosquito screen over the windows. Hawker guessed that this was where Curtis lived, his one concession to his past as a civilized man.

As they walked, the odd smell again drew Hawker's attention. He looked up at the side of a rock precipice, and there, for the first time, he saw the source of the sour odor. There, on staves, baking in the tropical sun, were heads. Human heads. Dozens and dozens of them; hundreds of human heads, each on its own pole, mostly men, but there were women, too, and even, it seemed from the distance of a hundred yards, children. The heads all faced the little military compound, the eyes sometimes wide-open and hollow, the mouths thrown open into wild, silent screams.

Hawker came to a stop, staring.

Colonel Curtis looked at Hawker, looked at the hillside, then back at Hawker. "Oh, you've spotted our trophy case, huh?" He laughed. He gave Hawker a slap on the shoulder that was harder than a friendly slap. "Don't let it bother you, Mr. Hawker. Or can I call you James?"

Hawker said nothing but continued to stare.

"James it is, then," Curtis rambled on. "I guess a sight like that is a little hard to handle for someone fresh from the outside world. 'Barbaric,' they would call it; indeed, as if those lily-fingered hypocrites have the right to call anything we do down here barbaric. They with their factories that are poisoning the earth and their politicians who would sell their mothers for a profit, or their weak-kneed military leaders who no longer have any appreciation for the battlefield. Instead they prefer to incinerate whole populations from a nice sanitary plane six miles high—and they call me barbaric. It's absurd!"

The pitch of the man's voice had risen perceptibly, and his eyes had taken on a pale, haunted look. Hawker caught Curtis's eyes for just a moment. It was like looking into two embers from hell.

"It is a little absurd," Hawker heard himself saying.

The colonel looked surprised for a moment, then threw back his head and laughed. "By God, you agree with me!" He slapped Hawker on the shoulder again, this time not as hard. "I *like* you, James. I like everything I've ever heard about you—and you might be surprised at some of my sources. And now to find out that you agree with my thinking . . . well, by God, it's just music to these old ears. Shit, this is a day for celebrating! But first we've got to pay a neighborly visit to our commie friends. After that we'll break out the palm wine and the *kashiri*, have the boys roast the tapir, have ourselves a good talk, then I'll assign you a nice young girl to relax you before lights-out. How's that sound?"

"Actually, Colonel, a talk with you is all I came for—"

"Hell," Curtis boomed, "don't be shy around me, boy! Stroll over to the mess there and grab yourself some tortillas and beans. Get a good shot of water, too, because it may be a while before you get time for another drink. Then I'll have one of my men fix you up with weapons. I want you to get a firsthand look at how we operate!"

With that, Curtis left him and began shouting orders at his troops. He used a mixture of Spanish and English, Hawker noted, and when he spoke, his men jumped.

Hawker took a last long look at the rows of screaming heads on the hillside. Seeing them made the rancid odor seem even stronger. Even so, he walked over to the open-air mess. If he was going to survive in this hellhole, he would have to eat. Bluebottle flies buzzed around the huge cauldron of beans. The stack of tortillas also sat open to the flies. Hawker found a stainless-steel bucket of fruit. He selected two avocados, a small pineapple, a stalk of half a dozen tiny bananas, and two or three other fruits he didn't recognize. He walked over to the shade of a tree, sat down, and began to eat.

"You *are* hungry."

The woman stood before him. She had changed into military khaki, like the men. Hawker noted that the pants were too big for her, and she wore lieutenant's bars on her field cap.

"Two or three pounds of fruit a day keeps the doctor away." He bit into a bright yellow orb and made a face. "This is sour as hell. What is it?"

The woman smiled. "It is *bacuri*. We use it for flavoring our drinks."

Hawker tossed the small fruit into the bushes. "You ought to put it in those pinto beans. Maybe it would keep the flies away."

She sat beside him. "You are angry. Why? Colonel Curtis seems so happy after his meeting with you. He says that you understand each other. He says that you will be friends. Isn't that true?"

Hawker broke open the pineapple and began to eat. It was delicious: sweet and pearlike, less stringy than those from Hawaii he had bought from stores. He said nothing.

"Why do you not answer me?"

"Because you made me promise not to judge him too quickly."

"You do not like him?"

Hawker motioned to the hillside without looking. "Let's just say I wouldn't hire him as my interior decorator."

The woman nodded and looked at the ground. "That is why I warned you. I knew . . . I knew it would be a shock to you. But for us, we who have lived with him these years have come to accept his ways."

"The ways of a madman?"

"He is winning this war for us! Before him, we were a poor band of rebels without organization, without hope. He has brought order to our cause, he has brought many victories! The government forces are terrified of him. Within a few months, he says, we will take Masagua City, the capital. The communist government will collapse and we will be in control!"

"Curtis will be in control, you mean. Lady, I am no fan of communism, but I'm smart enough to know that any man who lops off heads and decorates his camp with them can't be much better."

"You said that you would not judge him too quickly."

Hawker nodded. "That's right."

"You must stay with us at least a week."

"I will stay with you for however long it takes me to make up my mind. I keep thinking about what Curtis's people are doing back in the States. I have heard that his men in Georgia are torturing people, blackmailing people, to get enough money to run this little army of yours. For a time I didn't think it was true. Now I'm not so sure. I'm going to ask Curtis outright if it is true. He might be nuts, but I think he's so convinced in his righteousness that he'll tell me the truth. And, if it is true, I'm going back to the States to stop them."

The woman stood up. "It will be that simple?" she said, a touch of sarcasm in her voice.

"Stopping people is what I do best, Lieutenant."

"But you forget one thing, James."

"What's that?"

Turning to go, the woman said over her shoulder, "You forget that you cannot leave until we say that you can go."

EIGHT

Curtis led a band of fifty men and a few women out into the jungle in the late afternoon.

Hawker had tried to blend into the group, but Curtis insisted that the vigilante travel on horseback at the head of the column so that the two of them could talk.

"You see," Curtis said, pointing at the bruised thunderheads forming above the high canopy of jungle, "that is our cover. In guerrilla warfare a force must take advantage of all the disadvantages nature offers. In a rain forest we try to attack under the cover of rain. The government forces don't like rain. They are soft and spoiled by comforts. The rain wrinkles their nice dry clothes. It gets into their boots and gives them blisters when they march." The American laughed gaily. "But my men love the rain. It cloaks our noise, and it is a natural camouflage. A security guard can't see much when there is rain dripping into his eyes."

Overhead, the black clouds swirled like smoke in the tops of the great trees. There was a blinding flash of light, a *boom* that shook the earth, and then the rain began to fall.

Hawker had never seen such rain. It fell out of the trees not in individual drops but in a deluge, a river of water pouring off the huge jungle leaves.

To talk now, Curtis practically had to shout. "The government forces are looking for our camp," he said. "We have covered the trail, laid false trails, but even so, ultimately they will find it."

"Then why don't you wait in ambush?" Hawker called back.

"Because that is what they expect us to do. Certainly that is what *they* would do. But you see, James, the key to our success is the unexpected. All modesty aside, I must tell you that they have no military leader who possesses my background, my knowledge of practical warfare. That is why we are beating them. Beating them damn badly, I might add. I have used all the important elements of guerrilla warfare: surprise, mobility, and terror. Yes, terror is an important factor in this kind of war. I will admit that in my first year here I was reluctant to take the necessary steps. For instance, I saw the enemy as only the men trained and employed as government troops. It took me a little while to realize that our enemy was anyone—absolutely *anyone*—in this country who did not pick up arms and follow me. That was the key; that change in my thinking is what has produced all of our success. For me, fighting was really more of a complex seventeenth-century duel between two honorable gentlemen. The British made the same mistake during our own revolution, the Marines almost made it against the Japanese during the Second World War, and our entire political establishment made the mistake during Vietnam. There can be nothing honorable about guerrilla warfare."

"Does that same philosophy hold true for your men back in the States, Greg Warren and what's-his-name Pendleton?"

"Shawn Pendleton—and you're goddamn right it holds true!" Curtis snapped, swinging around in his saddle. "They have been sent back to Georgia to do a job, and they will, by God, do that job at any cost!"

"Even if it includes extortion? And blackmail? And murder?"

Curtis's face was growing red beneath the bushy gray eyebrows. "There's no such thing as blackmail and murder in this kind of war, friend. There is only victory. Or defeat. Don't you understand? *There are no rules!* That is what the loser learns but always too late! In this kind of war you must do anything, absolutely anything, that is necessary to win!"

"I wasn't aware that there was a war going on in Georgia," Hawker replied calmly.

Curtis laughed more to himself than to anyone. His eyes were glassy. "Wherever you find Captains Warren and Pendleton, friend, you are going to find some kind of war," he said. "They are my two best men. I hated to part with them, hated to send them back to the world. But it had to be done. I ran out of money more than a year ago. My so-called friends, the cowards, decided to stop contributing to the cause because of some nasty little stories they read in one of those left-wing pseudo newsmagazines. So that left us without money. No money source at all. The American CIA wouldn't offer a dime. They back every other gook, chink, and rebel sand nigger in the world, and they wouldn't chance a dime on an American who has already proved that he can win. So what were we supposed to do? You need money to run a war, friend. Lots of it. So I decided that if my rich friends wouldn't contribute voluntarily, we would make them contribute. I knew that wouldn't be easy to do, so I sent my two best officers. Pendleton and Warren both have their heads on right. They had their heads on right long before me; hell, they knew all about how to win—*really* win—long before they even came to the jungle. When they first got here, they did things that turned my stomach. Things to women and children in the villages that made me want to vomit. I warned them twice, then I brought them up on court-martial charges and found them guilty. All the other men were afraid of them. I decided to carry out the execution myself. So I tied them up against a tree and drew out my service revolver. You should have seen them. The two of them just sort of stood there looking at me, a kind of weird smile on their faces. Pendleton, he's a great big son of a bitch. He called out to me, 'Don't make a mess of it, Colonel. Shoot straight, damn it!'" Curtis banged his fist on his saddle and looked at Hawker. "That's when I *realized*. It was like something popped in my head, like a bright light. It was an awakening! I knew in that moment that both Pendleton and Warren had been right all along. They were the only two in the whole fucking camp who knew how to win this war, and here I was, about to shoot them. Hell, I was the one who should have been shot! Shot for incompetence! I was telling my people to fight a textbook war in a type of conflict that is fifty thousand years old. There is only one true path to victory in such a war: the path of terror! I untied Pendleton and Warren, promoted them both to captain, then asked them to help lay out an entirely new course of action in our war against the communists. Within a week we had our first great victory. We have had nothing but victories since."

"And you don't mind that the innocent people of Georgia suffer so that you can win a tiny war two thousand miles away?"

Curtis looked at him oddly. "Are you saying that I'm wrong?"

The pale eyes bored into Hawker, and he knew that how he answered would be the difference in his own life or death. Curtis's hand rested uneasily on the grip of his .45 automatic pistol. Hawker carried his own Beretta in the shoulder holster in plain view, and slung over his back was an M16 with a full clip he had selected from the camp arsenal. The vigilante didn't doubt that he could kill Curtis where he sat, if need be. But he also knew that Curtis's men would shoot him down before he had a chance to kick his horse into full gallop.

Hawker saw in the colonel's eyes that his very life depended on how he answered.

Trying not to cringe at the lie, Hawker said, "Wrong? Hell, no, I don't think you're wrong, Colonel . . ." And in his mind he continued, *I think you're as crazy as a bag lady, but I don't think you're wrong.*

Wellington Curtis threw back his shaved head and laughed loudly. "God damn it, Hawker, you had me worried there for a minute. I thought maybe you had come down here to put together information on my operation so you could go back to the world and squeeze Pendleton and Warren." The man's gaze grew sharp once again. "By the way, James, why *did* you come here?"

"To tell you the truth," Hawker said easily, "that was the reason I did come—to stop you and to stop your two men in Georgia."

Curtis roared at that. "If you have given me any other answer, James, I'd have known that you were lying. By God, I'm happy as hell that you've decided to join us. Let's see how you do in this first skirmish, but I think I can guarantee you a pretty fair rank after the way Laurene said you handled yourself during the attack on the plane this morning. Say, major?"

"Major? That's awfully generous of you, Colonel," said James Hawker. "I'm very honored . . ."

They forded the river into Masagua and marched another three miles before Curtis called the troops to a halt. The rain had abated; sheets of storm, dragging the gray tentacles of a squall, sailed across the distant hillside. In the green valley below was a village of thatched huts, camp fires, laughing children, barking dogs, women washing clothes at a stream.

"You expect to find the government troops here?" Hawker asked.

"Not at all," said Curtis. "I told you that we always try to do the unexpected. We slid past the government troops an hour ago, not long after it started to rain. You never noticed, did you? Ah, but I knew. I could smell their cooking; I could smell the very stink of their sweat. Our two armies probably passed within half a mile of each other. If you stay in the jungle long enough, your senses become so acute that you can tell such things accurately. As I told you, they were looking for our camp. By now they have found it. You noticed the tree houses we had built high up in the trees? The government troops will walk into an apparently deserted camp. When they are sufficiently close, my men in the tree houses will open fire with automatic weapons and grenades. We even have two shoulder-held rocket launchers. The soldiers they do not kill will flee in a panic. Those soldiers who survive will return to their base and tell the other soldiers horrifying stories about our hill of heads and how our weapons are far superior to theirs—the last, of course, will be a lie. But they will need to tell lies to save face, and that's all the better for us. A childish people, these Masaguans."

"That still doesn't explain why we have come to this village," said Hawker. "I don't understand."

Curtis swung down off his horse and unshouldered the automatic rifle from across his back. "This morning, James, when you were attacked at the airplane, you proved that you are not afraid to fight. This afternoon I want you to prove that you are not afraid to do what is necessary to win."

"You are going to attack the village," said Hawker.

"Exactly. I do not know that those people are sympathetic with the soldiers of the government. But it may be so. At any rate, my propaganda people will say that it is so in the leaflets they will print and distribute all around the country. And they will say that it is so on the broadcasts from our pirate radio stations up in the hills."

Hawker felt his stomach roll. "Why did we even bring weapons? I don't see any men down there."

"Of course you don't. This is the time when the *rabalo negro* spawns, the black snook fish. The men are all out on the river near the sea netting them, to be dried later by the women. Our propaganda people, of course, will decide that the men that were not in the village were off fighting with government forces. The men that remained behind, heavily armed with the most modern weapons, fought like cowards, for they held no true faith in their cause."

"But that's all a lie," said Hawker.

"Have you not learned anything from the American journalists?" Curtis almost shouted. "Facts may be used any way one wishes to get one's point across. Besides, I do not deal in lies or in truth. I deal in only one thing, James—victory! Now, are you going to help us or not?"

Hawker got down off his horse, thinking, *How in the hell am I going to warn those villagers in time?* He said, "I came to help, Colonel. Just tell me what to do."

"That's the spirit, man!" Curtis turned and called for his rebel troops to gather around him. "This," he said in Spanish, "will be our plan of operation . . ."

NINE

A plan to murder fifty unarmed women, children, and old men doesn't have to be complex to be successful.

This one wasn't.

Curtis picked a squad of eight men to maneuver around to where the village backed up against the next hill. From there, upon a prearranged signal, the squad would open fire, driving the occupants out of their huts and into the village's center green. Beyond that was the small river where the women now washed clothes. Curtis knew that the women and children would try to cross the river to safety. Once they were slowed by the water, the rest of the troops would attack.

Curtis referred to the rest of the troops as the "machete brigade."

Hawker realized that he had almost no chance of saving the villagers. But he did know that his only chance to escape might be during the confusion of the initial attack.

After that, Hawker was sure that Curtis would keep him

closely guarded until he was absolutely certain that Hawker was on their side.

And James Hawker knew that that day would never come.

"Colonel Curtis," Hawker said as the man dismissed his troops.

"Yes, Major Hawker—I think I can call you major now, don't you?"

"Ah, thank you very much, sir. But I wanted to ask a favor of you."

Curtis looked at him shrewdly. "Oh?"

"Yeah. I was hoping you'd let me go with the eight-man strike force."

Curtis thought for a moment. "You are that anxious to prove yourself to us?"

Hawker sensed a trap in the question. He shook his head. "I'm not going to bullshit you on this, Colonel. The truth is, I really can't see myself lopping off kids' heads. I mean, it may take a while for me to get used to that sort of thing. I don't mind being the first to attack the huts, though. It's possible that these people have the means to fight back. That makes it seem a little more fair, and it'll be easier on my conscience." Hawker paused, as if he were a teenage boy asking his father's advice. "Does that make sense to you, sir? I'm not a coward, and you've convinced me that what you're about to do is necessary. But, damn it, I just don't want to do it. Not yet, anyway."

Wellington Curtis smiled and wrapped his arm around Hawker. "I know exactly how you feel, boy. Hell, it took me nearly a year to get my mind on right. I thought that Pendleton and Greg Warren were animals at first, remember? You want to go with the attack force, you just go right on ahead. Sergeant Miles? Miles, get your ass over here!"

Sergeant Miles was one of the rawboned American men, little more than a teenager with blond hair, freckles, and light blue eyes. "Sergeant, we've got a little change in plans here."

Standing at attention, Miles said mechanically, "Sir! Yes, sir!"

"Mr. Hawker will be going along with you. He has the acting rank of major, and you will treat him as a superior."

"Sir! Yes, sir!"

"However, Sergeant, you already have your orders from me concerning our attack on the village, and those orders will stand. Understand?"

"Sir! Yes, sir!"

"Take good care of Major Hawker, Miles. If anything happens to him, it is your ass, boy. Questions?"

"No, sir. I understand, sir!"

Curtis smiled. "One more thing, Miles. See to it that Major Hawker is given a weapon that works. One of my subordinates insisted that he be given a dummy until we were sure of his intentions."

Hawker felt the sweat bead on his forehead but said nothing. If he had actually tried to escape earlier, he would have been dead in a second, his head left to the vultures on the hill of skulls.

So the vigilante followed Sergeant Miles and seven other American soldiers through the jungle on the two-mile journey to the other side of the hill. As they chopped their way through the bush, one scene stuck in Hawker's mind, a scene that had taken place just before they had left. Curtis had called Laurene Catacomez to his side. Then, with a glance as if to make sure that Hawker was watching, he pulled the woman roughly to him and kissed her brutally on the lips while his meaty left hand pulled the buttons of her blouse away, found her bare breast, and massaged it roughly.

Hawker expected the woman to recoil, if only briefly. She did not. Her eyes immediately rolled back, her face went slack, and her hips lifted to meet Curtis's. She was not shocked, not surprised. This, Hawker could tell, had happened before. Maybe it was a pre-battle ritual. A quickie in the bushes with his slave troops watching, just before the slaughter started. There was something wild, feral, in the demonstration: the bull male joining with the most desirable female to prove his dominance, to prove that he controlled the herd. And the woman was all for it.

The colonel's whore, she had called herself. She had not been lying. She was the colonel's property, body and soul. She had loaned herself to Hawker as an amusement.

Now convinced that it had been Laurene who insisted that he be given a dummy weapon, the vigilante turned away grimly, determined to do whatever he had to do to escape this band of savages.

As they made their way to the back of the village, halfway to the next hill, Sergeant Miles dropped back to the end of the line beside Hawker. An awkward, wary silence built between them before Miles finally spoke.

"So you're joining us?"

"Looks like it," Hawker said simply.

More silence.

"I'm kind of surprised, really," Miles said in a softer voice.

Hawker looked at him carefully. "Why's that?"

"It's just that I can't see why any outsider, especially from America where this kind of shit doesn't go on, would want to get involved."

There was something in the man's voice that interested Hawker. "You're fighting for a good cause, aren't you?"

The man shrugged. "If you call killing women and kids a good cause, yeah."

"You don't approve, Sergeant?"

"I don't approve or disapprove. I'm a soldier—or was. Marines, a chopper pilot. I came over here to fight communism. Turns out I'm fighting nothing but women, kids, and dirt farmers. But I still keep my weapon clean and do as I'm told."

Hawker slowed to let the other seven men draw ahead. He decided to take a chance. "Do you want to know what I really think, Sergeant? I think Wellington Curtis has gone totally insane. He's not a soldier, he's a butcher. And someone needs to stop him."

Miles stopped cold. "I could shoot you for saying that. In fact, that's exactly what Curtis told me to do. He said he didn't trust you. He said to feel you out, find out what you really thought."

Hawker's hand grew tighter on his M16. Was this another trap? Had they given him another dummy weapon?

"So what are you going to do, Sergeant?"

Miles thought for a moment, then began to walk again. "I think the two of us are going to get the hell out of here. Together."

"Just like that?"

"Two men could make it, Mr. Hawker. You don't know how many nights I've lain awake thinking about it. About exactly how to do it. One man wouldn't have much of a chance. But two men would. Two men could leap-frog their way into Masagua, covering each other's asses. Curtis would sure as hell send a hit team, and one man couldn't stay awake long enough to outlast them. Then maybe steal a canoe or something and paddle down the Rio Espiritu. It's supposed to have a couple of rough sets of rapids, and one man alone wouldn't fare too well. That river goes through some pretty remote shit too. Headhunter country, I hear. Little dark men who tie their dicks to their stomachs and use blowguns. No way you want those little bastards to catch you sleeping. The Espiritu comes within fifteen miles of Masagua City. There's a shitty little jetport there, and we could buy ourselves through customs onto a plane to Guatemala City or Bogota, then Miami. But we need money. Good American money. I don't have a cent. Curtis took it all when I arrived. That's another reason I need a partner."

Hidden in his belt Hawker always kept ten one-hundred-dollar bills. In his pocket, in traveler's checks, he had another five hundred plus change. "Yeah," said the vigilante, "I've got money."

The sergeant stopped walking again and faced the vigilante. "What do you say, Mr. Hawker? You want to give it a try?"

"Why didn't you pick one of your buddies to try this plan on, Miles? You don't know me. Curtis could have stuck me in here as a plant."

"That's right, he could have. But I feel a hell of a lot safer risking the idea on a stranger than on the guys here. Curtis has most of them brainwashed. Hell, they're as crazy as he is. Nobody trusts anybody else around here. Everybody is a spy. *Everybody*. You fuck up in Curtis's camp, friend, and public whipping is the best thing that can happen to you. That punishment covers everything up to slouching in the chow line. You do anything worse than slouch and the next punishment is public beheading. I don't know about you, Mr. Hawker, but crawling around in the dirt while my neck squirts blood ain't my idea of a dreamy way to die. I mean, this place really sucks, but why take unnecessary risks? I think there're probably other guys in camp who feel like I do. They'd love to get the hell away. I mean, I *can't* be the only one who wants to puke when I think about the . . . the women and kids I've killed. But everyone is afraid to discuss it, even when we're alone, for fear somebody will squeal."

"Yeah. I see what you mean, Miles. So when would you want to go? Tomorrow? Next week?"

"Next week? Shit, we need to get the fuck out of here *now*, Mr. Hawker. I mean, immediately. I wasn't kidding when I said that Curtis doesn't trust you. He told me so himself. That lady of his, Laurene, we call her the black fucking widow. See the way Curtis took her into the bushes back there and started humping her? They do that before every battle. Right out in the open. Curtis taps her on the head, and her fucking pants fall down, man. She gets off on blood and violence and shit like that. Never misses a beheading, that bitch doesn't. Probably gets her jeans all wet just thinking about it. She's the one who told Curtis not to trust you. You can bet on that."

Hawker tried to reconcile the tender moments he had had with Laurene Catacomez and the picture of her Miles now painted. He couldn't. He said, "We're not particularly well prepared for a long trip through the jungle, Sergeant. Between us we have two canteens of water, and that's all." The vigilante watched Miles carefully to see how he reacted, to see how serious he was about escaping.

The sergeant's face became animated. "We don't need anything else, Mr. Hawker. Hell, I've got my survival knife. And we've both got weapons. Curtis trained us on how to survive in the jungle. Shit, he may be as nutty as Ma Brown's muffins, but that old fuck knows his business when it comes to guerrilla fighting and survival. It should only take us about three days to get to Masagua City, and we'd have no trouble at all living out there for three years. There's food and water every place you look, man."

Hawker nodded. "Okay, Sergeant, you're on. We escape. Today."

"Not just today, Mr. Hawker, *now*."

The vigilante shook his head. "Leave, knowing that Curtis is going to butcher the people in that village? No thanks, Miles."

"But there's no way you can stop them, Mr. Hawker. Not and survive, anyway."

"Aren't you in charge of this squad?"

"Well, yeah, but I've already had my orders from Curtis."

"Did your men hear the orders?"

"No . . ."

"Sergeant, Curtis's orders just changed . . ."

TEN

From beneath the giant Guanacaste trees on the hillside Hawker could look down into the village. They were much closer now, only three hundred yards away, and he could see the people clearly. In the center of the village a clatter of boys, all ages, played a game with sticks and a leather ball. They shouted and wrestled and laughed. Naked toddlers, brown as the earth, scampered after the gang, not quite fast enough to keep up. Hawker could smell the wood smoke from the cooking fires, and women sat in the shade weaving or tending the food or carrying buckets to and from the river.

Sergeant Miles said to the seven men crouched around Hawker, "Gentlemen, this is Colonel Curtis's friend, Major Hawker. He is now in command of this mission. You will obey him as you would obey the colonel. Is that clear?"

"Why didn't Colonel Curtis tell us that," shot back a dour, weasel-faced American. Hawker had noticed the man before: greasy black hair, ragged battle dress, swastika tattoo on right forearm; a dope smoker who didn't even try to hide the cigar-size joint he toked on during the hike. The vigilante glared into the man's glazed, dark eyes. "Since when does Colonel Curtis need to clear his orders with you, mister?"

The military bite in Hawker's voice set the man back for a moment. "Well, it's just that I think he should tell us—"

"I don't give a flying fuck what you think, mister," Hawker said, cutting in. "You aren't getting paid to think. You're getting paid to follow orders. And right now your orders are to shut the fuck up and do exactly what I tell you to do. Question?"

"No, sir."

Hawker looked from face to face. "Do any of you other men have questions?"

They avoided his eyes; no more questions.

"Good. Then listen up. Sergeant Miles and I are going to enter that village. We are going to do it quietly, under stealth, so that if any government troops are hidden in those chikees, we can take them by surprise. If there are troops, you will hear the firing and Sergeant Miles will set off a red flare. Upon seeing the red flare you will immediately attack. If there are no government troops, we are going to centralize the village population—bring them into one chikee or one common area. Upon our signal—a green flare—you men are going to enter the village and attack. But you are not going to charge down off the hill; you are not going to make noise. This is an exercise, gentlemen. Colonel Curtis will be watching you carefully from the other side of the valley. We want to see how well you do in a hand-to-hand attack situation. That means no firearms. Only knives."

"Only knives!" weasel-face sputtered under his breath.

Hawker gave him a searing look. "If Sergeant Miles fires a green flare, that means that there are no government troops, mister. It means that there are only women and children and old men in the village. It means that even without firearms it will be like killing fish in a barrel. Do women and children and old men frighten you, mister?"

"I . . . I didn't think of it that way, sir. When you put it that way, it sounds kind of fun."

"That's what we're here for, fuckhead—to make sure you have fun." Hawker had been squatting; now he stood. "Okay. It will probably take Sergeant Miles and me about twenty or thirty minutes to scope out the village. You men are not to move under any circumstances—repeat, under *any* circumstances—until you see a red or green flare. Understand?"

They understood.

Hawker nodded to Miles, and the two men headed down the hill. When they were out of earshot, Miles whispered, "We're not really going down to the village, are we? We're skipping out, right? Hell, that was a great idea, Mr. Hawker! With a half-hour lead they'll never catch us."

"Yeah, but we won't have a half-hour lead because I really am going into the village. You'll stop at the line of trees and hold my weapons. I don't want to scare anybody when I go in."

"And then what? What the hell are you going to do when you get down there?"

Hawker put the M16 on the ground and unbuckled the belt that held his canteen and cheap production military knife. "I'm not sure," he said. "I'm going to have to play it by ear."

Hawker *was* sure what he wanted to do, but he still felt

uncomfortable telling Miles. What if the sergeant's story were an elaborate setup? *At least*, thought the vigilante, *I can save most of these villagers. If I'm lucky.*

As Hawker walked into the village he forced himself to relax, put a broad, easy smile on his face, and let his arms hang loose, like some benevolent uncle coming to call. He took care to stay close to the circle of chikees so that he could not be seen from the far hillside where Curtis and his troops waited. As he did he confirmed what he had noticed on the hike over: the edge of the village drifted into the line of trees not far from the river. It would be the one exit not open to easy view. When the village dogs saw him, they came to attention, ragged ears held high, then set off the alarm, barking wildly. The stick-ball game stopped; infants ran; mothers stood to stare. From beside the cooking fire in the center of the yard, an old man stood. He wore a brightly colored serape, still wet from the storm just past. His eyes were milky with age; his face gaunt, sun-blotched. He couldn't have weighed more than a hundred pounds, but he walked fearlessly toward Hawker.

The vigilante held up his hand, feeling ridiculously like Tonto on the Lone Ranger.

"Buenos días, señor."

The old man said nothing.

"I have come as a friend."

The old man stared.

"Habla Español? Habla Inglés?"

He said finally, "For what purpose do you come to our village? You are not of these parts." The old man spoke the slow, formal Spanish of the mountains, probably heavily accented with Mayan, though Hawker did not know the language well enough to be sure.

"I have come to tell you of—" What was the Spanish word for danger? *Peligro?* Yes, *peligro.* "I have come to tell you of danger. To warn you. In the hills waiting to attack are soldiers, *guerreros.* You must take your people away. *Peligro grande.* The danger is very great."

The village women had collected behind the old man.

The old man gazed up into the hills, then back at Hawker. "Do you speak of the evil white man? Do you speak of his soldiers, the ones who take heads?"

"*Si.* It is the evil white man of which I speak. They will be coming soon. You must leave quickly."

"Why do you, an *Americano,* come to warn us?"

"Because we are not all evil ones."

"Yes, that is so," the old man said simply.

Hawker motioned toward the chikees that disappeared into the trees. "You must go now! That way!" Hawker pointed to the far hillside and to the hill behind where Miles waited. "The soldiers are there and there. To escape you must stay hidden. Send the *hijos,* your sons, back out to play. They must be the last to leave. The soldiers will become suspicious if everyone disappears at once. Are your boys brave enough to do such a thing? To wait until the women are gone, then to run?"

"Like all boys, they are not so brave. But like few boys, they do as they are told. It will be done."

"Is there a safe place where your village can hide?"

"Yes, not far, in a hidden cave, there is such a place."

Hawker took the old man's hand. "Please hurry. There is not much time."

"This evil man, the one who seeks heads, will he not now kill you?"

"Only if I do not kill him first."

The old man nodded his simple understanding. "Then I wish you luck, my friend. On such a quest you will need great good luck . . ."

Doug Miles blended into the jungle so well in his camouflage that Hawker jumped when the blond-haired sergeant stepped out into the path. "You all set? You warn the villagers?"

"Yeah," said Hawker. "Any movement from the seven up above?"

"No, that little tongue-lashing you gave Blake really put the fear of God in them. They won't move until they see a flare." Miles looked across the valley where the boys had resumed their game. "Why are those kids still out there? Hell, Curtis isn't going to wait much longer. In about five minutes, if he doesn't see our signal, he's going to shoot off that gun to signal us to attack. And when we don't, he's going to go raging in there like a brushfire. Those kids will be slaughtered."

"The women and old men are escaping now. When they're gone, the boys are going to run for it."

Miles whistled softly. "That's cutting it awfully close, Mr. Hawker."

"There's no other way. If all activity in the village stops, Curtis won't wait. He'll go right in to see what's wrong."

Miles shook his head. "I'll tell you, between the fucking

communists and Curtis, these people really get the peanutty end of the stick. Hell, all they want to do is live, work, and eat their beans at the end of the day."

"Yeah, I know." Hawker strapped on his webbed belt and picked up the M16. "We'd better get going, Miles. We've got a lot of ground to cover and not much time. Which way?"

"Straight up the mountain, Mr. Hawker. They won't expect that. They'll expect us to follow the valley back toward Guatemala. Since that's the closest civilization, that's where Curtis will expect us to head."

Hawker smiled. "You weren't kidding. You have thought about this escape plan, haven't you?"

"Every fucking night since the first week I was here," Miles said grimly.

"The first week?"

"Yeah, about ten months ago. Like I said, I came to fight communists. Instead Curtis stuck a machete in my hand, pushing me into the center of camp, and made me chop off the head of a little girl. Since that night I've spent every waking hour planning this escape. Maybe it's because when I'm asleep, all I ever dream about is that poor little child."

Hawker gave the big man a gentle push in the back. "Let's get going. If it makes you feel any better, Sergeant, you helped save a lot of kids today."

Miles brightened. "Yeah, that's true. Hey, you're right! Hell, I actually did something good today. Kind of makes up for it a little bit, doesn't it? Hell, we've got clear sailing from here."

But it wasn't clear sailing. Half an hour later, well up the mountain and out of personal danger except for the rapids of the Rio Espiritu, the headhunters, and the communist troops of Masagua, Hawker stopped to look down into the valley.

Later in his life the vigilante would often wish that he had never stopped, never looked.

But he did. A moment earlier the boys of the village had dropped their sticks and made a show of ending the game for the benefit of the soldiers who watched from the hills. Hawker knew it meant that the women were safely hidden, and now the boys would follow.

Calmly they trotted back toward the chikees as if to dinner. In truth, they would continue running until they got to the cave where their mothers were waiting. But most of the boys never made it to the cave. From out of the line of trees soldiers charged them, led by Wellington Curtis on his rangy white horse.

Just behind and to his left, on a brown horse, rode Laurene Catacomez.

Both of them carried swords.

Absorbed by the jungle, the gunfire was a distant, muted popping, like the sound of a distant woodpecker. But Hawker could see pale puffs of smoke as the weapons jolted in the hands of the toy soldiers, and he could see the small brown boys tumble, fall, and scratch their way toward the trees, toward safety, on their scarlet bellies.

In tandem, Curtis and the woman chased the running children, cutting them down with their swords. A small boy of about ten, weary from running, held up his hands to protect his face from the charging horses—and both of his arms were cut off at the elbows. Another boy took a slash from Curtis that cut him from the shoulder and deep into his chest, yet he continued to run—only to have his throat cut by the woman.

Hawker felt someone tugging at his arm, and it took him a moment to realize that it was Sergeant Miles. "Come on, Mr. Hawker, don't look no more. It ain't good for you to watch that shit. You'll have the bad dream like I got. Don't look no more, man."

"They're worse than animals," Hawker whispered, still watching in disbelief.

"They ain't worth your time, Mr. Hawker. Come on, it's just like you said—it's all behind us now. We don't ever have to come back to this goddamn place." The vigilante noticed only peripherally that the big man was crying, crying for the children who now fell in the far valley.

Hawker turned slowly away, his gray eyes blazing. "You're wrong, sergeant. I *do* have to come back. I'm going to go to Atlanta first, but someday soon I'm going to return. And when I do, I'll wipe every trace of Wellington Curtis and his people from the face of this earth . . ."

ELEVEN

Atlanta, Georgia

Even at nine A.M. the heat was beginning to dominate Atlanta. The sun rose over the red-clay counties of Elbert, Wilkes, Oglethorpe, then hit the glass and white-stone skyscrapers of Atlanta, the burned brick of the Underground with its plush shops and cutesy boutiques, the hard gray geometries of the *Journal and Constitution* building, the steel and aluminized windows of Ted Turner's empire, the asphalt streets, the concrete apartment houses, the slums and suburbs and colonial mansions of one of the South's most modern cities.

James Hawker stepped out of the canned chill of his hotel and climbed into an oven disguised as a bright yellow rental car. He rolled down the windows, turned the air on full, and by the time he had turned from Auburn Avenue onto West Peachtree, the car was sufficiently wind-blasted that he could roll the windows back up.

Not far from the Federal Building, which was across from St. Joseph Infirmary and Harris Park, Hawker matched the address of a nondescript brownstone duplex with an address written on a piece of paper. A small bronze plaque outside said that it was the office of Hale & Sons, Exporters, by appointment only, please.

Hawker knew it to be a safehouse operated by the CIA.

He parked on a side street, trotted up the steps, slowly rang the bell three times, then twice quickly. Games. CIA games. Everything had to be in code.

The door cracked, then was thrown open.

"James! By God, it's good to see you. Come on in!" Jerry Rehfuss, CIA operative and, once upon a time, Hawker's friend, greeted him warmly and ushered him inside. "Come on up to the office. It's cooler. This damn central air doesn't work worth a crap, but they've installed a couple of window units up there that will freeze your knees off. God, I'd forgotten how shitty it is working in the field. Washington's got me spoiled."

The vigilante followed the rangy, red-haired man up the steps. From the other offices he could hear muted voices, the plastic clatter of a computer keyboard, the *bong* and *ding* of a switchboard, the rattle of a printer, but he saw no one else; every door was closed.

Rehfuss's temporary office had a green steel desk and a vinyl chair and couch, also green. There was a photograph of the president and an American flag behind the desk.

"Very nice," said Hawker, not smiling. "Almost a little too plush for good taste."

Rehfuss laughed—laughed too hard—and recovered quickly when he realized that he was forcing it. "Same old

James. Same wicked sarcasm. Hey! You look pretty good. Senator Thy Estes told me you'd had a rough trip back. Said it had taken you about a week. You've lost some weight, but other than that . . . Hey, how'd you get that scar on your face? God, that must have taken twenty stitches—"

"Twenty-five stitches. I had a little canoeing accident."

"Canoeing accident? Jesus, you're lucky you didn't bleed to death."

"Some Indians found us, fixed us up. They put a splint on my friend's arm and some kind of poultice on this." Hawker pointed to the white welt of flesh on the left side of his face.

"But they didn't stitch you up—"

"There was a pretty good American doctor in Masagua City. Runs a tiny little infirmary on the back side of the town. He did it. Said there would hardly even be a trace of a scar."

Rehfuss was suddenly interested. "An American doctor in Masagua? We are damn short of operatives in that country. Of course, we're not supposed to be there at all, but we maintain a few connections. That doctor could be a real windfall. Why in the hell do you think he's there? Running from some kind of criminal charge, maybe? Or he could be a junkie—a lot of doctors get hooked on their own wares. He'd be a lot closer to the source down there."

Hawker simply shook his head. "I wouldn't know."

Rehfuss, uneasy, rubbed his hands together and assumed the friendly grin. "Well, what the hell. I'll have one of our people check into it. Geez, it's damn good to see you, James. You really do look fine, considering the shit you've just been through."

Again Hawker did not respond. He knew he did not look fine, because he had indeed gone through some shit. Sergeant Miles's three-day escape had taken eight days. The canoe or boat he'd planned to steal turned out to be a tiny hand-hewn dugout. The "few rapids" of the Rio Espiritu turned out to be a series of roaring torrents with crosscurrent swells the size of houses, all crammed between sheer rock walls. By the time they heard the falls—and they did hear it; even above the wild roar of the river, the falls sounded like a sustained train crash—it was too late to do anything about it. They couldn't have gotten to shore if they had wanted to, and if they had, there was no way to get up the cliffs. So they had gone over the falls. Miraculously Hawker wasn't knocked unconscious. He managed to grab Miles by the collar of the shirt and steer the two of them to a little beach at the mouth of a stream that fed into the killer river. There the irony of Miles's bad planning took a brighter turn. The fierce headhunter Indians he had described were not fierce at all. They were a mild, shy people whose males did indeed belt their penises to their stomachs. But they seemed less interested in the heads of the two strange white men than they were in healing their wounds. After a day of rest Hawker selected a larger dugout—for which he traded his fighting knife—and they paddled the rest of the way to Masagua City without incident.

But the eight days had been tough ones. Both men had gotten gastroenteritis from drinking river water, and it was impossible to eat or drink anything without immediately having to squat in the bushes. The gash on Hawker's face got infected—but not until they had spent two nights in a cockroach-infested hotel in Masagua City. Both mornings he awoke, he noticed that the dressing the doctor had sent to put on his face was disappearing. He finally realized that the cockroaches were eating it off during the night.

So the vigilante knew that he did not look fine. When he stared at himself in the mirror, he saw a sun-darkened, gaunt imitation of his old self. The most disturbing thing, though, was the hollow, bleary look in his pale gray eyes. They had a troubled, haunted look, so much so that looking in the mirror was like looking into the face of some stranger who had seen the depths of hell.

Hawker had seen those bleak depths, and he continued to see them in his troubled sleep: screaming children being hacked to death as they tried to run to their mothers.

In the vigilante's mind it was his plan that had killed the children. He was the one who insisted that they stay and play while the women and old men escaped. It had been his own attempt at cleverness that had brought them face-to-face with horror, face-to-face with what the old Indian man had described as the White Evil One.

There were better plans—a hundred better plans he could have used that would have saved the entire village. Hawker had thought of them all in detail during that long, brutal trip to Masagua City.

But he had thought of them too late. Now he had to live with his own guilt, his own inner Evil One.

Hawker tapped his fingers on the steel desk and said, "Let's cut the bullshit, huh, Jerry? Yes, I look fine and it's a nice day and the weather is hot and Washington has more comfortable offices for its top CIA operatives. But I'm not here to discuss that. I'm here to talk about two of Wellington Curtis's hit men, Shawn Pendleton and Greg Warren. They have been extorting money from the people of Georgia to finance Curtis's Masaguan guerrilla forces. They are also suspected in several murders, though nothing can be proved because the people they have been hitting on are understandably scared shitless. And if they can scare the people of Georgia, they can scare anyone in this world. So the state law wants them, but they can't get proof, and they can't get anyone to testify. The federal law wants them, but they can't prove a federal case, and if they could, they'd run into the same problems with witnesses. So they've involved your people because you have a little freer rein on how you move, how you attack. But since Jimmy Carter made it illegal for you to participate in any kind of assassination plot anyplace, anytime, for any reason—there's irony for you—the good people of Georgia are stuck with these ghouls unless you bring in someone from the outside. Isn't that just about the way things stand?"

Rehfuss's face had sobered. "I was just trying to make conversation, James. I wanted you to know that I really am glad to see you."

"Isn't that just about the way things stand?" Hawker repeated.

"Look, James, if that's the way you want it, strictly business between the two of us, then I—"

Hawker slammed his hand on the desk. "Jerry, I have spent the last year of my life running from your people. They have tried to shoot me, poison me, stab me, and burn me to death in my sleep. That really isn't a very pleasant way to live. Now, if you expect me to come in here all smiles—"

"That wasn't my doing, damn it!"

"You're saying that it wasn't your organization?"

"You broke the rules, James! You didn't play by the book! You're not a kid; you knew the risk you were taking when you went against our orders on the Iranian thing—"

"But now you want me back?"

"That's right, Hawker, we want you back. We want you back for this one job because you are the very best available at what you do. You are fast and strong and smart, and you are a cold-blooded son of a bitch when you need to be. And it is those same qualities that have made this organization a viable force in world politics. When we see a threat to this nation's security, we, by God, go after it tooth and claw. And when someone on our payroll jumps out of line, we come down on them with both feet. We make it hurt, because if we didn't, every bimbo and international psycho in the world would soon hear about it, and we'd be just a little weaker. And a little weaker. And it would go on and on and on. We drew the line, Hawker. You're the one who decided to step over it!"

The two ex-friends glowered at each other for a time until Rehfuss finally settled back in his chair. "I'm sorry, James," he said with a sigh. "I thought it could be different. I don't blame you for holding a grudge, but I swear to God that I did everything in my power to get them to leave you alone."

"Does that mean you're no longer offering me a shot at Curtis and his men?"

Rehfuss smiled. "No, it doesn't mean that at all. This is

business. We're willing to forget our . . . past troubles if you'll undertake and successfully complete this mission for us."

"And what do you want me to do?"

The rangy CIA operative did not blink. "You know who the problems are. I want you to eliminate them. And, of course, if you are caught before, during, or after the completion of your mission, the corporation will disavow any knowledge of you or your assignment."

"I'll need help."

"Name it."

"Weapons, for one thing."

"Tell me exactly what you want, and I'll have them delivered anyplace you say."

"And any information available on the whereabouts of Warren and Pendleton."

Rehfuss slid a new leather briefcase across the desk. "You'll find everything you need in there. Money too. Ten grand in tens, twenties, and fifties."

Hawker pulled the briefcase his way. "And when I'm done in Atlanta, I want to go back to Central America. I want to finish Curtis once and for all."

"If you take care of Pendleton and Warren, you will have finished Curtis. No money, no army. It's as simple as that."

"Not for me it isn't. Promise me that if I take care of this Atlanta business, you'll help me in Central America. I'll need help with fake passports, transportation, and safehouses and weaponry in Guatemala, maybe Belize."

Rehfuss thought for a moment. "Is Curtis really as crazy as they say he is?"

"Crazier. He has worms in his brain, Jer. But he's still as shrewd as hell. I'm going to need every bit of help you can give me."

"We have strong operations in both Guatemala and Belize. You'll get whatever you need."

Hawker stood. He hesitated, then held out his hand. "I'm sorry I blew up at you, Jer."

The big CIA man took his hand. "Hell, it's half my fault. Senator Estes told me yesterday on the phone that you'd changed. She didn't say how, but she told me to act just like you were the same old James Hawker, an old friend. She said you had had a very bad time in the jungle and that it would make you feel better if I pretended not to notice. I should have known better than to try to bullshit you. Christ, I was as jumpy as a cat when you came in here. I felt like someone trying to sell junk cars." He smiled slyly. "You want the truth, James? You look like warmed-over shit. You're too skinny, and your clothes don't fit. That scar makes you look like a fucking Nazi hangman, and your eyes have a weird, glassy look—how did that football coach put it?—like the lights are on but nobody's home. There, how's that?"

Hawker grinned. "Now that's what I expect from an old friend. Sincerity." He turned to go, then stopped at the door. "One more thing, Jer. In Belize a guy tried to execute a contract on me—"

"Sure, I remember your call."

"Big black guy with an island accent. Chip on his shoulder but a pro. Was he one of your people? You said you'd check for sure."

Rehfuss nodded slowly. "I checked. His name is Lorenzo Chiles. His friends call him Sweet Chiles. He has done some free-lance work for us in the past. Small stuff, stuff that doesn't take much planning or brains."

"Why is it that I suddenly feel offended that you sent him after me?"

"I didn't send him. Someone from the Counter Intelligence staff, Western Hemisphere Division, hired him. I'm with the OO division, Office of Operations. But I imagine that they sent Chiles after you because he knew Central America and because just about everyone else had failed."

"Oh. And is the contract still out?"

"I can almost guarantee you that it isn't. And if it is, it soon won't be."

"Almost guarantee?"

"That's one of the problems with you freelance people. You don't have a clock to punch, so you don't check in with the office as often as you should. If Chiles has checked in, he knows the contract is off."

"Maybe you could have the folks in Counter Intelligence send him a telegram."

"A telegram? Hmm . . . gee, I never thought of that . . ."

TWELVE

Hawker spent the afternoon in his hotel room resting, reading the material Rehfuss had given him. The carefully written reports went into the vigilante's mind in bursts of pure data:

Shawn Pendleton, 31, Caucasian male. Seven arrests: four assaults, one armed robbery, one rape, one DWI. One conviction: DWI, fined, released. 6'4", 220 pounds, black hair, brown eyes, missing two upper incisor teeth, wears dental plate. Occupation listed variously as mechanic, motocross racer, mercenary. Dishonorable discharge U.S. Marines 6-10-69, cowardice under fire in Vietnam. Member Hell's Angels; Member Atlanta Ghost Riders. Always armed, considered extremely dangerous.

Greg Warren, 33, Caucasian male. Five arrests: four drug-trafficking, one assault, no convictions. 5'11", 180 pounds, blond hair, blue eyes, tattoo on right arm (American flag with serpent); scar on back right hand. Occupation listed variously as chemist, mercenary, *Playboy* photographer. Dishonorable discharge U.S. Marines 6-10-69, cowardice under fire. Member Atlanta Ghost Riders. Always armed, considered extremely dangerous.

Hawker read each man's dossier carefully, storing away information. And he began to get a pretty clear picture of the two men in his mind: pseudosoldiers who couldn't make it in the real military. Motorcycle tough guys when they had a gang behind them; bullies to whom Wellington Curtis had now given a purpose, a reason to use their strong-arm methods on isolated small-business people of Georgia.

There wasn't much on their victims in the briefcase, but what there was, Hawker noted carefully. Apparently a few of the victims were banding together to try to fight back. The small group was being organized by a man named Andrew Watkins, a former U.S. senator who had returned to Atlanta and private legal practice after three terms in office. It suddenly dawned on Hawker how he had come to get involved with the Wellington Curtis case. Senator Watkins had probably somehow communicated his problem to Thy Estes, and Thy had contacted Hawker's friend, Jake Hayes.

The vigilante made a few notes, checked a phone number in the Atlanta directory, then stripped off his clothes. On the way to the shower he took a cold bottle of Stroh's from the little refrigerator room service had provided, then scalded and sudsed himself for fifteen minutes until a loud tapping at the door sent him scampering for a towel.

"Who is it?"

A woman's voice. "Mr. Hawker? Are we interrupting? If we are, I can stop back. I left a message, but the clerk said you didn't pick it up."

Hawker recognized the voice. He pulled open the door. Senator Thy Estes stood holding a briefcase; big round glasses perched on the bun of red hair; heavy breasts and trim hips primly covered by white blouse and green tweed business skirt and jacket; strong, mature face with high Loretta Young cheekbones and a strong, full mouth. She seemed surprised to see him and stammered, "Oh, James . . . er, Mr. Hawker. I really didn't think you would be in. The man at the desk said you *weren't* in. I was going to slip this note beneath your door." She held up the note for inspection.

Behind the senator stood a twiggy, bird-faced lady who was absolutely shapeless. She also wore business clothes, wire-rimmed glasses . . . and an embarrassed smirk. "I don't think you've ever met my secretary, Ms. Talis?"

As Hawker stretched to shake the little woman's hand he realized for the first time that he was wearing only a towel. "But I can see that you're busy, Mr. Hawker," Senator Estes went on awkwardly. "We can stop back—"

"Come on in. I'll get some clothes on."

"Don't bother"—the secretary tittered at this—"I mean, we don't want to rush you—"

"Now, Senator," the secretary said in a Midwestern nasal whine, interrupting. "If you have business with Mr. Hawker, you just go right ahead. We don't have to meet with the mayor's committee for another hour, and I can go on down to the banquet room and stall them a bit if need be. I mean it. Go ahead and have your talk with Mr. Hawker."

Thy Estes laughed in acknowledgment of the little charade and stepped into the room. "Thanks, Sally. Tell those stuffy bastards down there I'm out shopping for a new hat. That's all they think women do, anyway."

"I'll do that, Senator." The birdy woman came very close to winking. "And enjoy your meeting."

Thy Estes stepped into the room, kicked the door closed, and immediately fell into Hawker's arms. She was laughing. "God, I thought Sally was going to faint when you opened the door wearing that towel. You are, um, a very big man, and that is a very small towel."

Hawker gave her a kiss on the forehead, then on the lips. "Sorry, lady. You took me by surprise. I didn't know you were traveling with a friend."

"We got to the hotel early so Sally could help me go over some of the material the mayor's going to want to discuss. And I was going to practice my speech. But then the man at the desk told me that you hadn't picked up your message, and I began to worry. I wanted to make sure you were taking me out to dinner tonight—"

"Dinner?"

"Yes, and don't try to crawfish out of it. You are taking me to the Top of the Town. We are going to order expensive food and wine, and we are going to eat and drink and play lewd little games with our feet under the table while we enjoy the lights of Atlanta."

"You seem very sure of yourself, woman."

"It's because I am very sure of myself, man." With her arms still around Hawker she dropped her briefcase on the floor. She held her face up to be kissed, and when Hawker only grinned, she pulled his head down to hers and kissed him fully. Then she reached up and shook her hair free so that it swung down over her shoulders and face. There was a glint in her blue eyes. "Did you hear my secretary say that I had only one hour? One short hour? Only sixty minutes—"

"I heard everything your secretary said, lady."

Thy began doing something with her hands, and the white blouse she wore strained away, revealing her full breasts cupped within a sheer white, see-through bra. Her nipples were pale pink beneath the silky material, and Hawker slid the tweed jacket from her shoulders, and the blouse opened completely so that he could see the pale contour of her ribs and taut abdomen. "We don't have much time, Mr. Hawker."

The vigilante kissed the woman softly, then harder, as his hands slid up her sides and began to massage the soft weight of her breasts. He felt her shudder. "Then we had better get down to business, Senator. But first I have a favor to ask."

"Anything—in exchange for what I want from you."

"Why is it that you politicians always have to get something in return?"

She kissed him deeply, communicating her demands with her tongue. "Do you mind so much? Besides, I've agreed, and I don't even know what it is you want yet."

"I want a meeting with Andrew Watkins. I found his number in the book. Will you call him?"

The woman used her tongue to dampen Hawker's ear, neck, and chest. "I don't have to call him. I'll be seeing him this afternoon. At the conference."

"Then it's a deal. You can set up a meeting for tomorrow morning?"

The woman began to move her hands over the vigilante's body. "Um, you're such a hard bargainer."

"And you are so damn sneaky."

"Sneaky? Me? Little old Thy Estes? Come, sir, I have nothing to hide. See?"

The woman reached both hands behind her, a gesture that drew the bra so tight that it seemed, for a moment, that the elastic would break, then she unsnapped the bra and slid it off, and her pale breasts expanded, took natural shape, wide, full, heavy, pink nipples elongated and pointed upward. She began to sway slowly back and forth, rubbing herself against Hawker's chest, head tilted slightly back, eyes closed, as her hands now found the towel that Hawker was wearing and stripped it away. She looked down at him. "My God, James, how you've *grown.*"

They both laughed, and the vigilante swept the woman up in his arms as if carrying a bride across the threshold. She seemed surprisingly light as the vigilante carried her across the room to the bed. As he did he slid one hand up her skirt, felt the sheer nylon of her stockings, felt the garter-belt strap on the inside of her thighs—and noticed something else.

"Christ, Thy, you're not wearing any underwear!"

The woman smiled vampishly. "Since I've met you, James,

I've become a wanton woman. A damn wicked woman. I kept thinking of meeting you tonight at the restaurant and how I could surprise you, really please you. I decided to give you something to do with your hands while we were waiting for our food."

As she spoke, Hawker's hand moved high to the inside of her thigh, and he watched the woman's face go blank, eyes round, as he touched her, then slid his finger inside her, feeling the hot, smooth inner wall of her body. "Oh, God," she whispered. "Oh, God, that feels so good, James, and I want you so damn badly."

The vigilante dropped her onto the bed and slid the skirt up over her hips and began to torture the woman with his tongue as her hips lifted, wanting, demanding, pressing to satisfy her more quickly.

"Yes, James, do *that*, James, yes, yes, yes, faster, faster, *faster . . .* "

Hawker looked absently at his heavy Seiko diver's watch. He lifted his head and grinned. "Only half an hour until you have to get ready to meet the mayor and his committee, Senator."

"You really are a bastard sometimes," she said, groaning.

"I know the pride you take in being prompt."

She grabbed his hair, and the vigilante let her roll him onto his back. "And I know just how I want to spend the next half hour," she said, grinning back at him. The woman lifted the skirt up over her hips, straddled Hawker, used her left hand to position him, then slid down onto him, spreading her legs so as to take him as deeply as possible. "This is how I want to spend the next thirty minutes," she whispered, head thrown back, hair hanging, eyes closed in ecstasy. "All thirty minutes, James, please."

Already fighting not to spend himself too soon, Hawker pushed his hips upward. "Actually, twenty-nine minutes now."

Thy Estes lifted, thrust in return, lifted, thrust, lifted and pushed harder, faster, demanding. "Twenty-nine minutes," she moaned, "and counting . . ."

THIRTEEN

Andrew Watkins, former United States Senator, one of the wealthiest men in Georgia, and the leader of the small group of businessmen and farmers who were now trying to fight back against Wellington Curtis, lived in an authentic Southern mansion on the south bank of the Chattahoochee River. Hawker took busy Interstate 75 north, caught the bypass Interstate 285 west, then exited on the Johnson Ferry Road north into the red-clay country of central Georgia. There were flat fields of cotton shimmering in the heat; pine forests; wooden shanties with tin roofs; kids on bikes playing in sand yards.

Watkins's home was an oasis of Spanish-moss-draped oaks and green hedges. The mansion was down a long lane, a great white anachronism of the Old South: Roman columns supported the broad veranda with its brick floor, rocking chairs, hammocks, tables for bourbon and branch water; an upper balcony opened out from double doors from which could be seen the servants' cottage, the barn and pasture where horses grazed, the screened swimming pool, the bathing house on the Chattahoochee River as the river flowed swiftly toward distant rapids, green and silver in the sun.

Hawker went to the door, waited after the deep *bing-bong* of the bell. He expected Watkins to be of the new breed of Southerners, the Jimmy Carter type: soft, sophisticated, trendy, affected.

Hawker's preconceptions, to his great relief, were dispelled the moment Watkins opened the door.

"You Jimmy Hawker, the man Thy Estes sent to see me? Hey, come on out to the porch, boy. Set yourself down. That big red-haired lady give me a little more notice, I'd a worked up a good bass-fishin' trip so's the two of us coulda had something to do while we chewed the fat. Hell, nothin' fun about this type of meeting. Man who said you can't do two things at once was dumber than pig shit if you ask me. What you want to drink, boy? Go on, set yourself down." Andrew Watkins, ex-Senator Andrew Watkins, was all of five and a half feet tall, weighed probably a hundred and sixty, and he wore baggy, paint-stained khaki pants, a soft brushed cotton shirt of the L.L. Bean variety, Wellington boots, and an Atlanta Braves baseball cap. He had a broad, humorous face, sun-swollen nose, Clark Gable ears, and wide, shrewd blue eyes. Everything about him was at once relaxed but energized. Hawker realized with some amusement that in just the short introduction Watkins had established himself as Hawker's friend, leader, and confidant.

The vigilante took a seat in one of the wicker rocking chairs. "I'd like some iced tea if you've got it."

The older man made a face. "Tea? What are you, boy, some kind of Englishman? I got me some bourbon in there that's guaranteed twenty years old, smooth as a baby's bottom. Let me get you just a touch of that, how 'bout it?"

"Okay, Senator. Bourbon it is."

"That's the spirit. Never trusted a man that don't drink. 'Cept an alcoholic, of course. Admire the hell out of an alcoholic that give it up. An alcoholic who does that's got the balls of a junkyard dog. A regular dang saint, and I ain't kidding." The little man turned without warning and yelled, "Sarah! Sarah! Get your dark ass out here! We got company, goddamn it."

A moment later a handsome black woman appeared on the porch carrying a tray. Though she was probably in her early fifties, she had the long legs, trim hips, and body of a much younger woman. She was startlingly attractive with skin the color of pale wood, and she looked fondly at the little man as she said, "Yes, Senator, I have everything you need right here."

"Well, it's about damn time. Didn't you hear the door bell ring?"

The woman continued smiling. "Yes, Senator. That's why I got the tray ready." She crossed in front of Hawker. "Bourbon for you, Mr. Hawker. Andrew said that's what you would want"—she gave him a sidelong glance—"and, of course, he's never wrong. And here's a little carafe of water, straight from the spring. He said you might like that too. Can I get you a little something to eat?"

"No, ma'am, I'm just fine, thank you."

"See there, Senator? A man with manners. You might take a lesson or two."

"God, woman, don't be getting uppity with me in front of company. Just hand me my drink and get back to your duties. The damn garden's 'bout eat up with weeds, and them bastard sand-spur have taken over the backyard. You got fieldwork to do."

The woman handed him a tall, sweating glass topped with a twist of lime. "Now, now, Senator, let's watch our language. Here's your iced tea. I had the maid bruise some mint and add it to the water when she brewed it, just the way you like it."

Andrew Watkins made a face. "Goddamn it, woman, I ain't ever liked tea, and I ain't ever going to like tea. Keeps me jittery and makes me pee. Why in hell do you keep bringing me this crap?" He shook his fist at her, and it was only then that Hawker realized that the two of them were enjoying an old and private game. "I can't sell you no more, but I can, by God, fire your black ass!"

The woman leaned over and kissed him tenderly on the forehead. "Yes, dear. Now drink your tea. And after Mr. Hawker leaves the trash needs taking out."

Watkins was laughing softly to himself as the woman disappeared inside. "Women," he said. "God, what strange things they make us do." Hawker could only nod in agreement as the little man continued. "Twenty-five years ago Lester Maddox and me stood shoulder-to-shoulder at the restaurant holding ax handles to keep them Negro agitators out. I had plenty of good friends that was Negroes, but I believed that a man who owned a restaurant, who worked his ass off to keep it going, ought to have some say about who goes in and who stays out. Well, I still believe that, but things change, Mr. Hawker. With every bad change a little good sneaks right in with it. Them agitators had them a woman lawyer fresh out of Grambling. She was a beautiful thing to look at, and she could twist them Washington Yankee bureaucrats right around her little finger. They was anxious to feel guilty about bein' white, but they was even more anxious to get into that little girl's pants. She worked on their guilt without givin' away that other thing, and that one woman did more for the civil rights movement than all them Afro-haired dumb shits put together. And hate me? That woman hated me with a spittin' passion. Called me a Nazi on national TV. Brought suit against me in federal court and tried to have me disbarred. Campaigned hard for my opponent in the first election and cried like a baby when I won. Shit, she even snuck Tabasco in my drink at some damn convention and had an AP photographer hiding, ready to snap my picture. The cutline they used when they ran the picture over the wire was, 'Senator Watkins reacts to passage of busing bill.' Just about made me look like a fucking idiot.

"Well, that woman stayed in politics one way or 'nother, and we saw quite a bit of each other at parties and rallies and such, and we'd always compete to see who could be nastiest. The woman had a tongue like a serpent, I'm tellin' ya. Keep me awake at nights just so's I'd have something clever to say the next time we meet. She'd say something like, 'Well, Senator, if you disagree with me, why don't you stand up and speak louder so everyone can hear?' And, of course, she could see damn plain that I was already standing up. And I'd say stuff like, 'Counselor, when they give you that diploma at Grambling, how many professors you have to ask before you found one that could read it to you?' I mean, Mr. Hawker, we'd say *mean* shit.

"It got to be kind of a game. And after a time it got so we both looked forward to seeing each other to see who could nail the other to the wall. Our little jokes got harder and harder, but we were really liking each other better and better. Found out later that the dang woman was bribin' one of my secretaries so as she could find out what parties I was gonna be at and where. Well, one thing about a Washington party, it's filled with stuffed shirts, assholes, and journalists— a journalist being a pretty even cross between the two, only they're more prone to drug use. At those kind of parties you got to watch what you say every minute. Can't trust nobody, so nobody has any real fun, except the journalists, of course, 'cause they're drinking free booze and using their drugs over in some corner, and nobody's gonna squeal on them, 'cause who would write the damn story? Well, got so this woman and I would spend most our time together at these parties 'cause, hell, we'd both said just about every nasty thing in the book to each other and didn't have no need for soft talk or bullshit. A person you can speak plainly and honestly to, Mr. Hawker, is a rare commodity these days. In Washington, D.C., a person like that is a regular damn auk. We both appreciated the break, you might say.

"So when I retired from the Senate, I hired this woman into the firm. It was a damn smart move on my part, 'cause it got us a lot of the black business in Atlanta, and if you haven't noticed, boy, there's a considerable population of those folk. Well, my wife, God bless her, passed away, and then I got into some personal trouble and, fact is, needed a woman. Only woman I could trust was this damn Negro agitator. She helped me more'n most of my white friends would've or could've, and that was her what just brought you your bourbon."

"Sarah?"

"Miz Sarah, I call her."

"How long since you've had a drink, Senator?"

Watkins chuckled. "You don't miss a trick, do you, boy? I ain't had a touch since thirteen months before Miz Sarah and me got married. It was the one stipulation she made: I had to stay off the Tennessee tonic for at least a year or she wouldn't have me. We got married three years ago." The little man smiled. "It ain't easy being an alcoholic, Mr. Hawker. I still buy the bourbon for my friends, and I like to make sure they drink it, 'cause I buy the best and I, by God, love the smell of it. But being an alcoholic has helped me in a lot of ways too. For one thing, quitting the booze has given me one hell of a lot of respect for myself. It wasn't easy, especially 'cause I was never really convinced that I was an alcoholic until I'd been dry for about three months. Another thing, it's helped me to understand other people's problems better." The senator looked up at Hawker shrewdly. "And that's why you're here, ain't it, Mr. Hawker? 'Cause some folks in these parts got troubles?"

"That's right, Senator."

"Ol' Thy Estes is a real frank lady. Usually has no trouble speakin' her mind, but maybe you already know that, huh? Well, she told me that she trusts you one hundred percent. And she said that you could help us. But the weird thing is, she wouldn't say how. And you know what, Mr. Hawker? I don't want to know how. The law has become a strange thing these days. The more they legislate, the bigger the holes in the laws become. All kinds of reasons why bad men can't be put away. All kinds of legal reasons why hardworking, honest people have to put up with shit that no civilized people should have to put up with. I'm not interested in how you help us, Mr. Hawker, I'm interested in results. And Thy Estes says you produce results."

"I try, Senator."

"Good, boy, that's good to hear. Well, I'm a plainspoken man, Mr. Hawker, so before we even get started, tell me how much this help of yours is going to cost."

"No cost, Senator. Not a penny. All I need is information."

The little man's eyes bored into him, and in that moment Hawker saw beneath the easy-talking, good-ol'-boy facade of Andrew Watkins. He saw a tough, shrewd man and a cold, calculating intellect. Hawker wondered how many times the humorous facade had trapped his associates on the Senate floor and how many times those same associates had been made to squirm when Watkins turned that cold gaze on them. "You don't charge nothing? Don't want no kind of compensation or special favors? You just doing this out of the kindness of your heart, right, boy?"

"That's right, Senator."

Watkins pushed the baseball cap back on his head. "Son, I've had business dealings with white men, black men, Eskimoes, Indians, Chinese, and two or three kinds'a midgets, but I ain't met anyone who would do something for nothing. Now what's your angle, boy?"

"No angle, Senator. You're thinking I might get rid of one problem, then become a problem myself, correct? Well, you're wrong. I'm not a shakedown artist, and I'm not a con man. Am I doing this out of the kindness of my heart? Almost never. But this case is an exception. I've been with Wellington Curtis in Masagua. I know what he is doing down there. He is slaughtering people. Not communists, not government troops, but villagers who have little more than sticks to fight with.

"Have you read his book, *The Killing Tree?* I have. I finished it last night. In it he writes about effective guerrilla warfare. He says that a guerrilla army, properly trained, can take control of an entire country with only an occasional direct firefight with opposing forces. The way to do it is through intimidation, through wholesale slaughter. Sooner or later, he says, the citizenry will have had enough and force their own government to relent.

"Of course, when he wrote the book, the idea was repugnant to him. But something happened to him in the jungle. He got caught up in it; he went insane. Shawn Pendleton and Greg Warren liked slaughtering people, and they helped him along. Now, when the government forces of Masagua attack his people, he retaliates by wiping out a defenseless village. He hacks down women and children and hangs their heads on a hillside for public display. He has thousands of heads, Senator. I've seen them.

"So what do I want to be paid? Nothing, Senator, not a damn thing. I'm taking this job because I want to. I am going to cripple Wellington Curtis's operation. And then I am going to eliminate Wellington Curtis."

The older man whistled softly. "Mr. Hawker, when you get angry, you get a look in those gray eyes of yours that is purely like a nightmare. You ain't mad at me about my little cross-examination, are you?"

Hawker realized that his hands were clenched into fists. He relaxed them, smiling. "No, Senator. But I would like some information on Pendleton and Warren. I've heard that you've formed a group to try to resist their shakedowns."

Watkins sat back in his chair and rocked. "Ain't much of a group, really. Mostly made up of folks who know the victims. The victims themselves are too damn scared to go to the law and too damn scared to fight. Pendleton and Warren match right up with your story about Curtis. From what I gather they are regular animals. They go to rural cotton and tobacco farmers, small businessmen, and they ask for donations to Curtis's little army. If the folks refuse, they come back later and kick the shit out of the man. If they still refuse, they go after the woman. Rape her, if she's pretty enough, cut her up if she's not. Not many refuse after that, but if they do, or if they threaten to go to the law, Pendleton and Warren threaten to kill the kids. Real slimy characters, those two. They put the folks on a monthly donation plan. If the money keeps coming, the beatings stop."

"So what's your group done so far?"

"Not much. When we get wind of a new victim, we go and offer whatever help we can give. Try to convince them to go to the law. But when a man's kids are threatened, he's going to do everything in his power to keep 'em safe. And that includes keeping his mouth shut. So we keep chewing at the ass of the authorities to lock up those two bastards. No luck so far."

Hawker thought for a moment. "Have you heard about any new victims? Anyone who Pendleton and Warren might favor with a return visit?"

Watkins nodded. "Matter of fact, there is. Over Blackshear way, little town 'bout forty miles from here, there's a young couple got a cotton/tobacco dealership. Jon and Cathy Sanders is their names. They buy, sell, and rent warehouses. You know the sort of thing. 'Bout two weeks ago I heard that Jon got the living bejesus kicked out of him. Wouldn't tell the law nothing. He's got a couple of kids, not even in school yet, so it adds up. I got in touch, and he wouldn't tell me no thin', either. I told him I knew who did it, but he said he'd handle it himself. Jon's a good boy. I knew his daddy. But he is purely scared to death that if he squeals, them two bastards are gonna come back and kill those kids." The senator looked up. "He ain't gonna tell you nothing, either, Mr. Hawker."

"He doesn't need to, Senator. But the next time Pendleton and Warren come around, I'll be there—if you'll help."

Watkins turned unexpectedly and yelled, "Sarah! Damn it, Sarah, where the hell are you? Lazy damn coloreds! Mr. Hawker needs hisself another bourbon, woman!" The senator looked back and grinned, holding up his glass of iced tea as a toast. "You're goddamn right I'll help, boy—on the one condition that you come back here someday and we go out bass fishin' where there ain't no likelihood of wiretaps or bugs, and you tell me without leaving out a single bloody detail just what you did to them greasy bastards."

FOURTEEN

The dirt parking lot of Sanders & Sanders tobacco warehouses was illuminated by a single mercury vapor lamp. The lamp, from its high aluminum pole, threw a cold light over the outdoor auction booths; the loading ramps; a big new corrugated steel building; a smaller, dilapidated wooden building; the corner of a tobacco field with its broad-leafed plants that trailed away into darkness, shadowy in the pale glow of a quarter moon.

Except for one car in the parking lot—a Ford station wagon that had just pulled in—the place was deserted.

The car was owned by Jon Sanders, who waited alone inside the warehouse, unaware that, outside, the vigilante watched over him from the shadows.

James Hawker sat in the high limbs of an oak so big and old that it had probably been standing in the days when General Sherman marched his army through to Atlanta. Across his back was slung a short-barreled Colt Commando submachine gun. Strapped in the shoulder holster outside his black Navy watch sweater was a Smith & Wesson .45-calibre ACP. Attached to the webbed combat belt were five grenades, a pouch of plastic explosives, a UHF radio, and plenty of ammunition. Belted to Hawker's calf was his Randall Attack/Survival knife, Model 18.

The Randall had saved the vigilante's life more than once.

He was ready. And now he waited.

Waited for the vehicle he knew would bring Shawn Pendleton and Greg Warren to their meeting with Sanders, a meeting in which Sanders was to pay them five hundred dollars in protection money, his "donation" for the month.

The vehicle also brought them, Hawker knew, toward their rendezvous with death.

With the help of Senator Watkins, Hawker had spent two weeks in the little town of Black-shear. He had spent the days familiarizing himself with the area, learning the roads, but mostly resting and working out and honing his plan to destroy Wellington Curtis and his organization.

On his first night in town, staying in a cottage owned by one of the senator's friends, Hawker had gone to the road outside Sanders's pleasant rural home and found the telephone terminal. It was one of the tubular ones into which ran underground cable and drop lines.

Staying in the shadows to avoid the occasional passing truck, Hawker used a test set—a rubber-coated, hand-held telephone with alligator clips—to find Sanders's line. It was not difficult. He kept clipping onto pairs and dialing Sanders's number until he got a busy signal. When he hung up, the phone rang inside the house. Hawker was close enough to hear it. He watched a pretty woman carrying a baby cross behind the front window, and she answered the phone.

"Hello?"

"Sorry, ma'am, this is the phone man," Hawker said. "We had a report that some of your neighbors were having trouble, and we're just checking this cable."

"We haven't been having any trouble until just now. The phone's been making real short rings, but when I answer, no one's there." The woman had a soft Southern accent that was touched, Hawker noticed, with a little edge of anxiety.

"I'm sorry, ma'am, that was me."

"Well, shouldn't you be doing this a little earlier in the day? You woke up my little girl."

"I really am sorry, ma'am. All the complaints we've been getting have been at night, and we thought the dew might be causing a short. You know, only at night 'cause we couldn't find a thing wrong during the day. I think I've got everything cleared up now. I stuck in some temporary pairs, used some open colors, so you might notice that your reception isn't quite as good. But it's only temporary, like I said. No need to report it. We'll get new cable in just as soon as we can."

"I have no idea what you're talking about, sir, but I'd greatly appreciate your not calling so late anymore."

"Yes, ma'am, I'm real sorry to trouble you."

So Hawker had connected a tiny, two-wired transmitter to the line—it would blur the reception of the inside phone slightly—then drove five more miles toward his cottage where he climbed a telephone pole and, on the very top of it, mounted a Walkman-size relay that would boost the signal of the transmitter and send it cleanly the next six miles to Hawker's cottage where he had a tape recorder set up with a sound-activating device tuned to the proper frequency.

Hawker installed the same kind of transmitter and booster on the business line that fed into the warehouse office.

Now he could monitor all calls that Jon and Cathy Sanders received.

All there was to do then was wait. Wait until either Pendleton or Warren contacted them and demanded more money. Or wait until they made their whereabouts known to him. And Hawker knew they would.

So thirteen days went by without a lead; thirteen days of listening to Cathy Sanders talk to her mother, her pediatrician, her brother in Athens, her sister in Tupelo; thirteen days of listening to Jon Sanders buy, sell, and deal in tobacco and cotton. And in each of their voices, clear on the recorder, was a tightness, an anxiety, a remoteness that told Hawker clearly enough that they were living in fear. For the young couple every morning brought another day spent in hell. Their money was being drained from them. And the lives of their children were in danger. And there wasn't a thing in the world they could do about it.

Hawker wondered how many other couples in Georgia were living in the exact same kind of terror because of Pendleton and Warren.

Then finally the break came.

On a Wednesday night the telephone at the Sanders's house rang.

"We gonna be making our monthly collection Friday

night, Mr. Sanders," a deep, soft voice said. There was a long silence. "Mr. Sanders? You there, ol' buddy?"

Hawker recognized the voice of Jon Sanders. "I'm here. How much do ya'll want?"

"Let me see now, five for your kind donation, plus another single for expenses. Six to make it a nice round figure."

"Last month it was only five."

"Last month was last month, friend. You do what you damn well want. But you know what's going to happen if you don't produce."

Sanders's voice was weary. "I'll produce. When and where?"

"Let's say the warehouse. 'Bout ten P.M."

"I'll be there."

"And so will I," Hawker had whispered to the tape recorder after hearing the conversation.

Now, from the boughs of the oak, Hawker had a clear view of the warehouse and of the long dirt road that exited off the main highway, three miles away. Farther in the distance he could see the lights of two or three rural farmhouses sparkling in the distance.

The tobacco warehouse was remote; far from anyone who might hear his assault on the Curtis gang. It gave him more latitude on how to attack, a hell of a lot more latitude.

At nine-thirty P.M., sure that Pendleton and Warren were not going to be early, sure that they had not posted lookouts on the roads earlier, Hawker climbed down from the tree and walked to the warehouse. Through the dusty window he could see Jon Sanders. Sanders was hunched over his desk, head in his hands. Hawker tapped on the door and watched the man start.

"Door's not locked!"

Hawker stepped in and saw the surprise on Sanders's face. "I got the money. No need for you to come armed like that."

"I didn't come for the money, Jon," Hawker said softly.

Sanders had a lean Nordic face and pale sandy hair. He took a step back. "You didn't come to beat me, did you? A man can't stand another beating like that last one they gave me. Besides, like I said, I got the money."

Hawker held his hands outward, palms open. "I'm not here to hurt you, Jon, and I'm not with Pendleton and Warren."

"Then who in hell—" His face grew even more worried. "Jesus Christ, you're not a policeman, are you? I'm telling you, mister, if you're a policeman, just get the hell out. Now! I mean it. They'll kill my little boy and girl. They will. Even if you arrest those two, they got plenty of others working for them. And I ain't having my kids' heads cut off like that little boy in Marietta and those two little girls down in Macon. The police figure that it's some crazy child molester, but I *know* who did it. The daddies of those kids tried to get help. Well, I ain't asking for any help, mister, and I ain't taking any help. It ain't worth risking the lives of my children."

Hawker continued to speak softly, confidently, trying to instill calm in the man. "I'm not a policeman, Jon. I'm a friend. I know exactly what I'm doing, and I'm going to help you. But first you have to let me help."

"I'm not going to endanger my kids—"

"Your children are going to be just fine, Jon. I promise you that. Trust me."

"Trust you, hell! I don't even know you."

"There's the phone. Call Andrew Watkins." Hawker held out his palm where he had written the number. "There's the number. Go ahead, we don't have much time."

"Senator Watkins?"

"Jon, if you want to spend the rest of your life living in fear, I'll leave. But if you're tired of it, if you want it all ended tonight, call."

Sanders hesitated, then picked up the phone. Hawker waited, then smeared the numbers on his palm after the man had dialed.

"Hello? Senator Watkins? This here is Jon Sanders up at—Oh, you were expecting my call? The reason I'm calling is—" Sanders's face became quizzical, and he put down the phone. "All the senator said was that the reddish-haired man can be trusted completely. He gave me his word of honor. Then he hung up."

Hawker lifted his black watch cap enough for Sanders to see his hair. "So now will you do as I say?"

"But what are you going to do when those guys get here?"

"You don't need to know what I'm going to do, Jon. All you need to know is what you're going to do. You're going to get on the phone right now and tell your wife to pack a bag for you and the kids. Tell her to phone her brother in Athens and tell him that you're coming to spend the night—"

"How'd you know she's got a brother in Athens?"

"It's my business to know things, Jon, but you're wasting time. When you get home, you are going to load the car immediately, and you are going to drive to the first open gas station. There you will refuel, buy snacks, whatever you need, and make sure you strike up a conversation with the attendant. Can you do that?"

"John Knight or his son, Billy, are usually at the Esso station till midnight."

"Good. Talk to them. Make sure they remember you. Tell them your house is being fumigated in the morning and that you have to spend the night in Athens with your brother-in-law. Mention the time to him. Tell him your watch is off and you want to check his."

"But my house isn't being fumigated."

"Yes, it is. I arranged it all, paid for in advance. They'll be at your house early tomorrow. You won't be able to move back in until the day after tomorrow, and you decided at the last minute that it would just be easier to drive over to Athens tonight. Tomorrow afternoon give Senator Watkins a call. Ask him how things are going. If he says everything's just fine, it means it's safe to return to your house. If he says he's been feeling a little tired, stay in Athens. He'll be in touch and will help you make arrangements for a safe place to stay until this thing is all cleared up. Do you have all that, Jon? It's important that you do exactly as I say."

"Well, yes, I guess so . . . but are you sure you should be doing this?"

"I'm sure, Jon. And one more thing: What's inside the old wooden building next door?"

"Nothing, really. Junk. Trash. We're going to have it razed in early September when the heavy rains start."

"Good. When you leave, turn out the lights here and lock the doors. Does the old building have lights?"

"Yeah, it's got lights."

"Then turn on the lights in there and leave the doors wide-open. Got it?"

The man nodded.

"Then get going, Jon. Now."

Hawker stepped back outside and began to let the door close, but Sanders called after him, "Hey, wait!"

"Yeah?"

"Just who in the hell are you, anyway?"

"A friend, Jon. Just a friend."

Hawker found a hiding place in a clump of bushes. He watched Sanders lock the corrugated steel building, watched him open the wooden building, flick on the lights, then drive off.

The vigilante waited . . . waited . . . urinated onto the grass . . . waited some more.

At ten-twenty P.M. he saw car lights approaching. Then another set of car lights.

Damn, he whispered.

Two fast cars skidded around the bend and roared into the parking lot: a big dark Cadillac and a gaudy new pickup truck on giant tires.

Four men got out of the Cadillac. Three got out of the pickup. Several of them carried sawed-off shotguns, others handguns. Of all Hawker had read of Pendleton and Warren, of all he had heard—and it wasn't much—he'd had no idea that they were traveling with a gang.

There were seven of them, seven big, heavily armed, dangerous men. And Hawker was going to have to find a way of dealing with all of them.

The tallest of them, a huge, solid man with shoulder-length black hair wearing combat boots and fatigues, Hawker immediately marked as Pendleton. In his right hand he carried what looked to be a small metal box with a tube sticking out of one end.

The vigilante recognized it for what it was: an Uzi submachine gun.

From the driver's side of the pickup a smaller man with shoulder-length blond hair got out. He immediately took charge. It was Warren.

"Two of you men stay with the vehicles," he ordered. "Josh, you mosey on back down the road a hundred meters or so and keep your eyes open for visitors. We don't want no surprises. If you see something suspicious, give me two shots. Got it?"

"Got it!"

"The rest of you boys come with Shawn and me. Keep your weapons on safety. We shouldn't have any trouble with this guy."

"But, Greg, there's no car here. Hell, you think he even showed up?"

"After he read the news stories about them two little girls in Macon, you're damn right he showed up. He's inside that building. Hell, he probably crawled on his belly—that's how scared the little shit is. And if he's not here, you can damn sure bet he'll be pulling up any minute."

Hawker watched the men separate—something about which he was not pleased. It was now impossible to take them all by surprise.

He watched two of the men position themselves by the

cars, a third walk alone into the darkness of the dirt road, and the other two follow Pendleton and Warren into the building.

Quickly then, Hawker formed an alternate plan. None of them could escape. None of them could leave alive, for it would mean that Jon Sanders and his family would live under a shadow of fear for the rest of their lives.

No, he had to kill them all. And he had to do it quickly, effectively, and, in the beginning at least, quietly.

Quickly the vigilante slung the Colt Commando back over his shoulder. Then the vigilante pulled up the cuff of his jeans and drew the cold, heavy weight of his attack knife . . .

FIFTEEN

Hawker moved quietly and quickly along the ditch at the edge of the dirt road.

He held the knife low so that its polished blade would not glimmer in the moonlight.

Ahead, still walking slowly down the road, he could see the dim outline of the gang member. The man carried the sawed-off shotgun over his shoulder, barrel in hand, like a duck hunter after a long day in the field. Hawker watched as the man slowed at a clump of trees, then took a seat beneath a large oak.

The vigilante angled away from the road and into the tobacco field. On his belly and elbows he began to crawl toward the tree.

The tobacco plants smelled slightly sour, touched with some kind of chemical odor like pesticide.

Every few minutes he would poke his head up above the plants to see exactly where he was. When he was behind the oak tree, he began to cut across the rows, made his way silently through the bushes, then halted there for a few moments, waiting.

The man still lounged against the oak. He kept humming to himself, snapping his fingers occasionally, and it took the vigilante a moment to see that he had the tiny foam earphones of a Walkman clamped over his ears. He was listening to music, and in his right hand he held a tiny, torpedo-shaped cigarette. Hawker could smell the sickly sweet odor, and he knew that it was marijuana.

Calmly the vigilante stood, holding the knife at hip level. He tried to remember if he had ever killed a defenseless man so cold-bloodedly.

No.

But this wasn't just any case. This man was part of a gang that beat innocent men and women; a gang that, by Warren's own admission, had been responsible for the deaths—the beheadings—of two children in Macon and probably a third child in Marietta.

Yes, this case was different. Hawker knew that to succeed he had to be just as brutal, just as merciless as Curtis and his gang.

The vigilante took two slow steps toward the tree; he waited. Still the man did not move.

Calmly, coldly then, in one swift, sure motion, he grabbed the man by the hair, yanked his head back, and swept the razor edge of the attack knife across the man's throat, through the plasticlike gristle of his windpipe.

The man kicked on the ground wildly, neck pouring blood, eyes wide-open, hands clawing at his throat, then lay still.

The vigilante cleaned his knife on the grass, holstered it in the leg sheath, then trotted back toward the warehouse.

Six more to go.

It had taken him just over seven minutes to stalk and kill the first guard. He knew that inside the warehouse Warren, Pendleton, and the other two men would be getting antsy, tired of waiting on Sanders.

It was a delicate problem. If he attacked the two guards at the cars, he would certainly be heard, and then the other four could barricade themselves in the old building and Hawker would be in for a dangerous firefight.

If he entered the warehouse from behind and attacked the four men inside, the two guards would have plenty of time to either join in the fight or, most probably, escape to take revenge at a later date.

Hawker decided to take the surer, more time-consuming—and dangerous—route.

As he neared the pickup truck and Cadillac, the vigilante began to slow his pace. He could see the two men clearly, standing shoulder-to-shoulder, talking. He held the stubby Colt submachine gun down so that it matched the movement of his leg. With his right hand he pulled a thermite grenade from his belt.

When Hawker was thirty yards from the vehicles, they finally noticed him, finally noticed that it was not their comrade coming back from his post on the dirt road.

"Hey—hey! Who the hell are you?"

Hawker pulled the pin from the grenade and rolled it

under the pickup by their feet, at the same time lifting the Commando to hip level in his left hand. "I came with a message from Curtis," Hawker said quickly.

"Hey, he just threw a fucking grenade!"

"Curtis said he'll see you in hell!"

Hawker squeezed off a quick burst before he dived for the ditch; saw one of the men get knocked off his feet as the slugs drove through his chest, saw the other trip backward in shock and pain; then the grenade exploded, and the two vehicles and the two men were consumed in blinding white fire that raged so fiercely, it sucked the screams from their lips.

Hawker stood. The thermite burned at more than two thousand degrees, and the heat was wilting.

He stood behind the flames, submachine gun ready, the black watch cap pulled low over his head, his angular, unemotional face glistening with sweat.

He'll see you in hell!

Those two are already in hell, the vigilante thought. *My hell. And now the rest are going to join them . . .*

Immediately the front door of the old warehouse smacked open and the two men who had been with Warren and Pendleton stuck their heads out. Hawker saw their eyes grow wide with horror as they saw their two companions on the ground, their bodies ablaze—and the vigilante froze the look of surprise on their faces when he opened up with another volley from the Commando.

The Colt's 5.56-mm. slugs burst their faces open like melons and catapulted them back inside the doorway.

In the warehouse windows shattered. Hawker ran in a serpentine sprint and dived into the ditch as automatic weapons fire pocked the red dirt at his heels.

"I'm going to blow your fucking head off!" came a wild threat shouted from the building.

Hawker answered back. "Pendleton! Warren! I don't want you two! I want Curtis. Understand?"

A long burst of weapons fire was their answer.

"All I want is information! Do you hear me? Show yourselves and we can talk!"

"Who in the hell are you?"

Hawker pulled a second thermite grenade from his belt and absently checked his watch. 10:47 P.M. By now Jon Sanders and his family should have already left the gas station and be well on their way to Athens, their alibi intact. There was no way in the world that the people on the adjoining farms could have missed hearing the explosion of the first grenade, and later the authorities would tie the explosion directly to the deaths of at least two of the men.

"You don't need to know who I am," Hawker called back. "All you have to do is answer my questions. Now come on out!"

Another hail of slugs smacked through the brush overhead. Hawker pulled the pin on the second grenade and tossed it toward the building, turning his eyes away from the blinding flare.

The old wood caught on fire immediately, wildly, in a popping, all-consuming blaze.

"We're going to burn to death in here!"

"Then come on out! Toss your weapons out and follow them, hands on the tops of your heads."

"You're going to kill us!" The voice was Pendleton's, and he was crying as he yelled, "You got to promise not to murder us!"

"All I want is information," Hawker yelled back. "Understand? That's all I want."

"You got to promise!"

Hawker almost chuckled at the childish whine in the man's voice. What was he going to say: Cross my heart and hope to die?

"Get your asses out here, you two pukes!"

The door of the warehouse swung open. One Uzi then another was tossed out, followed by Pendleton and Warren, hands on the tops of their heads.

Everything was as bright as day now, brighter in a wild, flickering golden light. Electrical wires popped and burst as the flames consumed the wooden building. Hawker slid a new magazine into the Commando, drew his .45 ACP, and walked slowly toward the two men.

Pendleton was standing nervously, shifting his weight like a child who had to pee. "You promised, you promised, you promised," he kept saying nonsensically.

"Shut the fuck up!" Warren, the smaller blond man, snapped at him. "He ain't going to kill us." He glared at Hawker. "Are you, man?"

Hawker thumbed back the hammer of the .45. "What makes you so sure—man?"

"'Cause we got money. Lots of money. We'll give it to you. We'll give it all to you."

"How much?"

"Sixty, seventy grand. And it's all yours. In cash."

"But it's Curtis's money. What's he going to say?"

"I don't give a shit what he says as long as you don't kill us."

"Why would you give the money to Curtis, anyway? Why wouldn't you keep it for yourselves?"

Warren's eyebrows raised as if surprised. "We do keep some of it. But the rest is small potatoes compared to what we're going to get, man. Hell, he's going to take over Masagua. He's going to rule it like a king. We're going to be his top men. Anything we want, any money, any property, any women, anything we want is ours. Hell, you could be part of it. We could tell Curtis that you helped us. What you make as a cop? Twenty grand a year? Hell, down there, when he takes over, you can live like a fucking sultan. Screw a different girl every night—"

"Shut up."

"You a cop, man?" whined Pendleton. "You a cop, sir? Please, we know our rights, sir. You got to take us in. You got to call us a lawyer. You got to read us our rights. Ain't that right, Greg?"

"You'll get a fair trial, sport. But first I want to know a couple more things. How do you get the money to Curtis?"

"We got a deal with a cargo company in Atlanta. They fly it direct to Belize City. Hell, they think we're shipping out drugs or something. But the customs people don't look for nothing going *out* of this country, just in. In Belize the customs people are on the take, anyway. Then Curtis's lady picks up the shipment, or I hire a small plane, depending on the load, and fly the guns and money and all direct to the base."

"And when are they due to pick up the next shipment?"

"It's up to us, always up to us unless they really need something special. I'd planned a shipment in about another week or two, I guess."

"And how do you let Curtis know you're coming? How do you let him know you don't want Laurene Catacomez to pick up the stuff?"

Warren hesitated just a little too long, and the vigilante slapped him with the barrel of the .45. He said, "I know a lot about the operation already, friend. Some of this shit I'm asking you are test questions. Others aren't. If you lie to me once, just once, I'll kill you and your friend."

"I'll tell you, mister," Pendleton cried, stepping forward. "I'll tell you everything. Greg sends him a telegram, sends it to a pimp he's got in Belize City. Says either, 'Pick up produce Monday two P.M.' or whatever the day is, or it says, 'Arriving with produce,' then whatever the day is."

"What's the pimp's name in Belize?"

"His name's Martin . . . Martinis. Thurston Martinis. At the Sea Beach Hotel. Martinis gets in touch with Curtis."

The vigilante thought for a moment. "You ever have a beard, Warren?"

"Well, yeah, why—"

"When's the last time Curtis saw you?"

"He ain't seen either of us for almost two months," Pendleton shot in.

Hawker nodded. "That's it, then. That's all I need to know."

Pendleton sighed and started to lower his hands. "We can go, then? You're letting us go?"

The vigilante shook his head. "No. But I'm about to give you your fair trial." From his belt Hawker took the UHF radio, switched it on, and hit the mike key. "Air mobile, air mobile, this is Almighty, do you copy?"

There was a squawk of static, and the voice of ex-sergeant Doug Miles came back. "I've got you, Almighty. Things all tidied up there?"

"Just about. You can come on in now and make it quick. Get the box of salt ready."

"Box of salt, that's a roger. Will do."

Hawker switched off the radio, put it away. Now Warren was getting nervous. "What was that box-of-salt business? I don't like that. What in hell are you planning to do?"

"Greg Warren," Hawker said in a formal voice, "are you responsible for the deaths of children in Macon and Marietta?"

"What? Hey, no, you can't ask me that. It ain't legal—"

"Shawn Pendleton, are you responsible for the murders of one child in Marietta and two children in Macon?"

Pendleton dropped to his knees, begging, a huge, blubbering baby with the face of a weasel. "I didn't want to do it. Please, please don't kill us, sir. It was Greg's idea . . ."

"You have both been as fairly tried as you deserve, and I now pronounce you guilty of murder in the first degree—"

"You son of a bitch—"

The .45 automatic jumped in Hawker's hands, making the familiar loud metallic clang with each ejection of spent cartridge as he shot them both, Warren in the face and Pendleton in the top of the head.

In the near distance the vigilante could hear the ceiling-fan thud of Miles approaching in the helicopter.

Calmly Hawker holstered the .45 and took out his knife . . .

SIXTEEN

A Rain Forest in Guatemala

On the grass landing strip the faces of two men stared blankly out of the cockpit of the little red Dakota airplane that James Hawker had hired in Belize City.

Hawker had sent a telegram three days earlier to Thurston Martinis. The telegram read: "Will deliver produce Monday, two P.M. Big load.

Now it was Monday. Now it was one thirty-five P.M. And the vigilante sat comfortably in the dank coolness of a towering Guanacaste tree while wild monkeys squawked and chattered overhead.

From his hiding place he could see the plane, could see the faces of the two men inside the plane, could see the landing strip and the mud road that led toward Curtis's camp.

He had been sitting in this spot for more than an hour, waiting. He had been sitting since he and Miles had finished the digging and planting and preparing it had taken to get ready for Curtis and his army.

The vigilante wore camouflage fatigues and greasepaint on his face so that no one could see him, not even Doug Miles, who, similarly dressed, was hidden on the other side of the landing strip.

Resting across Hawker's lap was the Colt Commando, barrel and folding stock scratched from rough use. Strapped to his hip was the Smith & Wesson .45. On the ground beside him was a metal can full of loaded clips for the Commando. Nearby were two electronic detonators, each with four individually wired toggle switches.

Miles also had a submachine gun . . . and detonators.

At 1:48 P.M. Hawker heard the first sign of their approach. The monkeys in the high trees began to scream their warnings, spooking outward, away from the mud trail.

Then Hawker could hear the clank-rattle-snort of horses pulling wagons in jungle heat and, later, the muted sound of a man's voice.

It was Wellington Curtis.

The vigilante fought the urge to stand so that he could get a better look. Any movement now might give his position away, might ruin everything.

Then Curtis came riding into the clearing, riding in on the ragged gray horse. He wore khaki pants, combat boots, aviator sunglasses, and a jaunty red beret on his shaved head. In the saddle scabbard appeared to be some kind of pump-action shotgun, probably a Winchester Model 12. Slung over his shoulder was an M16, and strapped bandolero fashion across his hairy chest were belts of ammunition. The squat, heavyset man held up his hand like a cavalry soldier, and his troops on foot and horseback halted behind him, about forty yards from the plane. Laurene Catacomez, her pretty black hair hanging down over her safari shirt, reined up beside him.

Curtis looked at the woman, said something, then he cupped his hands and yelled toward the plane, "Captain Warren, Pendleton! Wake up, you lazy bastards! You can sleep after we've had a drink together!"

Behind him his band of mercenaries chuckled.

Curtis waited and, when they did not stir, yelled again, "Warren, Pendleton, wake your asses up!"

Slowly, ever so slowly, the smile faded from the man's face. "Captain Warren? Captain Warren, I'm talking to you!"

Hawker could hear the woman's voice. "They're probably very tired, Colonel."

"Probably drunk, more like it."

Curtis kicked his horse into a brief gallop, reined up beside the plane, reached over from the backside of the wing, and yanked open the door.

Hawker had been waiting for this moment, anticipating Curtis's reaction. And he wasn't disappointed.

When the door was thrown open, the severed head of Greg Warren tumbled out, pulling along with it the stick on which it had been placed. It rolled across the wing, making a sound like a rotten melon, right into Curtis's lap.

The colonel slapped at it with a look of wild distaste on his face and finally grabbed it by the hair and flung it away.

Warren's head hit the fuselage with a thud, and the vibration caused Pendleton's head to pivot in the other seat slowly, eerily, staring wide-eyed, mustache salt-encrusted, directly at Curtis.

Curtis sat staring in disbelief, his chest spasming as if he had just had cold water thrown on him. "Jesus Christ . . . they're . . . they're . . . *Somebody cut their heads off!*"

He whirled away on his horse, then stopped cold. His eyes frantically searched the line of trees. He yelled to his troops, "Separate! *Dispersar, dispersar.* Meet at B Camp, Camp B!"

There were about seventy or eighty men. Hawker had seen them before, coming across the field that day when they massacred the boys of the village. This, though, was a different situation. The men saw the heads, and they knew what the heads meant. They meant that someone—probably government troops—waited in the trees, ready to attack. And these men were murderers, not soldiers, not fighters.

All of the men tried to run at once, on foot or on horseback. There was panic, chaos, much shouting, many collisions, but they finally began to move in a wild herd away from the plane.

The vigilante waited calmly, and when the troops were near enough, he picked up the detonator and flicked the first toggle switch.

There was a deafening explosion that brought grass and human debris raining down through the forest.

Overhead, the monkeys shrieked.

The men who survived sprinted away in the opposite

direction. On the other side of the clearing Doug Miles used his detonator, and there was another huge explosion.

Now the survivors scattered in all directions. One by one Hawker touched the other toggle switches and watched as the grassy clearing became a boiling inferno of dust, of flames, of quaking earth.

Then there was silence or what seemed to be silence: all along the far end of the landing strip, men lay scattered, a few of them moaning, as debris continued to clatter through the high canopy of forest.

James Hawker stood still. He had insisted that none of the charges be planted close enough to damage the plane—he wasn't about to spend another week with Miles fighting his way out of the jungle.

So now only the plane remained, and it was in the plane that Wellington Curtis and the woman had taken sanctuary. In that moment the vigilante realized his own stupidity. He had expected them to run with the others. But, of course, they wouldn't, because Laurene Catacomez was a pilot.

The red Dakota barked and shuddered, and then the single propeller began to blur.

Hawker was running. He raised the Colt Commando, knowing that he could destroy the engine or explode the gas tank with a long burst of fire—but then how would he and Miles get out?

The plane jolted, began to move slowly, and pivoted on the strip toward Hawker and the long expanse of open runway.

Hawker ran out into the middle of the field. From the corner of his eye he saw Miles lifting his rifle awkwardly in his one good arm. There was the muted clatter of fire, and dirt exploded near the landing gear of the moving plane. The plane jolted and swerved as one of the tires gave way, and now it was coming right at the vigilante, gaining speed despite the blown tire. Hawker could see Curtis and the woman clearly now, as if in eerie slow motion: Curtis's face a pasty mixture of fear and rage; the woman looking preoccupied, intense, as if concentrating on nothing more than getting the wounded craft off the ground.

The vigilante did not move as the plane bore down on him. Calmly he raised his submachine gun and brought the grooved sights to bear on Curtis's face. The little colonel, the war historian who had lost his personal war in the jungle, raised his hands as if to fend off a blow, but he was too late. Hawker squeezed off four single shots as the plane swerved to a halt, engine still running, only a few yards away.

Hawker jumped onto the wing root and pulled open the door. Curtis fell out onto the wing, then fell off onto the ground, bleeding badly from the neck and shoulder.

The vigilante looked down on him as his eyes struggled to open. "I am dying?" he whispered, but in an oddly clear voice. It was not the voice Hawker associated with the insane guerrilla leader. It was a softer, more refined voice, touched with the dignity of the Old South.

"Yes," said Hawker. "You are dying."

Curtis nodded as if in agreement, then his eyes closed for the last time as he whispered, "What took you so long, Mr. Hawker? What took you . . . so . . . long?"

Behind him, the woman stepped out onto the wing and

jumped down to the ground. She looked at Curtis's body for a moment, then looked up at Hawker. "I'm glad," she said, looking hard into Hawker's eyes. "I've wanted him dead for so long."

Hawker stepped down beside her. "Have you, Laurene? Have you really?"

She fell against his chest, holding him while Hawker stood icily, not looking at her, not touching her. "How can you believe anything else, James? That night we spent together, didn't you know then? God, how I hated that man! How I wanted to vomit when he touched me! I knew you were going to escape; I wanted you to escape, even though it broke my heart to know that we probably would not see each other again. But now . . . " Her dark eyes looked up into Hawker's, and he noticed again how beautiful her Latin face was. "But now that's all behind us, James. We've both been through hell, but we can start again. Start fresh, just the two of us."

"If that's the way you felt, Laurene, why didn't you leave Curtis earlier?"

She pulled away, her small hands squeezing Hawker's arms, trying to shake him to make him believe. "He had my brother, James! He would have killed my dear Mario—"

"But Mario *was* killed."

"Yes, but I haven't had a chance to escape since his death. Curtis knew I wanted to go, so he had me watched constantly after Mario's death. I think he always knew how much I hated him—"

"And how much you hated killing? I saw you, Laurene. I saw you and Curtis ride down into the village, hacking little boys to death. You thought I would be miles away, running. But I wasn't. I was sitting on the hillside, watching. And you know something else, Laurene? You enjoyed it. You enjoyed every second of it."

Slowly the woman's face changed. It changed from the mirror of breathless, frightened beauty into something bitter . . . tormented . . . vile; a snake's head on a beautiful woman's body. "You saw that, did you?" she said, her lips contorted. "Yes, then you know. Enjoy it? Of course I enjoyed it! You saw them as boys—I saw them as men. Pigs! The bastards! They play in the fields when they could be fighting for the return of our land. Were they not of Mayan blood like me? Yet their blood has grown so thin, so cowardly, that they are worthless. Worthless! Yes, I hacked them into little pieces, and I would do it again in a moment." Slowly she began to back away from Hawker. "They bowed down to men like Curtis. I said that Curtis made me want to vomit? I told the truth. For a time I thought it could be different with you. For a time it did *seem* . . . different; you with your muscles and your tenderness and your strange, quiet ways. But you are an *Americano*, like all the rest—"

Hawker stepped toward her. "Laurene, stop. It doesn't have to end this way."

From somewhere a snub-nosed revolver appeared in her hand, and she leveled it at the vigilante's face. "Doesn't it? Do you forget that time at the bar in Belize? I looked into your eyes then. I *knew* that you would kill Curtis but led you to him, anyway. I used you! I have used your filthy kind all of my life. A rich American bought me food and clothes, sent me to a school so that I could learn to speak properly and not embarrass him. A fat American kept me until I was old enough to live on my own—he taught me to fly. Curtis helped me wage war; war the way it should be waged. And always the price was my body, and that was a fair price to me because I love the feel of a man inside me. Any man! I have always used your kind, and I have always hated your kind, and in the end I have killed each and every one of you, just as I now must . . . must kill you!"

"Is that the way you saw it that day in the bar, Laurene? That you would kill me?"

Her eyes softened for just an instant. "No . . . but that is the way it must end. Not the other way; it can't end the other way."

Hawker took another step. "You need help, Laurene. Let me try to—"

"No! Not another step. I must kill you, I must, or—"

"Freeze, bitch!" Doug Miles had come limping around the tail of the plane, his submachine gun half raised. Frightened, the woman jumped. Then, with the same look of surprise on her face, she got off two quick shots and Hawker dropped backward to the ground, and then she turned to sprint away . . . and ran directly into the moving propeller of the plane.

"Jesus," Miles whistled softly as he knelt over Hawker. "Did she hit you?"

The vigilante got shakily to his feet. For some reason he couldn't take his eyes off the thing that had once been a woman. "What? No . . . no, she didn't hit me. That close, I don't see how she could miss."

Miles sat down heavily and began to massage an obviously

swollen ankle. "Me, neither, Mr. Hawker. I've seen her shoot before. She's one hell of a shot"—he looked in the direction of the dead woman—"or was, I mean. She almost had to *want* to miss not to hit you at that range. Either that or she wasn't seeing too clearly."

James Hawker picked up his submachine gun and began to walk toward the fresher air of the rain forest. "I don't know," he said without emotion. "Maybe she saw too clearly for her own good . . ."

ABOUT THE AUTHOR

Randy Wayne White was born in Ashland, Ohio, in 1950. Best known for his series featuring retired NSA agent Doc Ford, he has published over twenty crime fiction and nonfiction adventure books. White began writing while working as a fishing guide in Florida, where most of his books are set. His earlier writings include the Hawker series, which he published under the pen name Carl Ramm. White has received several awards for his fiction, and his novels have been featured on the *New York Times* bestseller list. He was a monthly columnist for *Outside* magazine and has contributed to several other publications, as well as lectured throughout the United States and travelled extensively. White currently lives on Pine Island in South Florida, and remains an active member of the community through his involvement with local civic affairs as well as the restaurant Doc Ford's Sanibel Rum Bar and Grill.

THE HAWKER SERIES

FROM OPEN ROAD MEDIA

INTEGRATED MEDIA

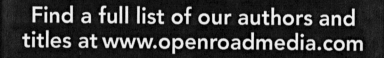

Find a full list of our authors and
titles at www.openroadmedia.com

FOLLOW US
@OpenRoadMedia

CPSIA information can be obtained at www.ICGtesting.com
Printed in the USA
BVOW05s0905220416

445237BV00001B/7/P

9 781504 035224